Hotel du Lac

Modern Women Writers

Series editor: Maura Healy

The *Modern Women Writers* series is part of the
Longman Study Texts   General editor: Richard Adams

Anita Brookner

Hotel du Lac

edited by
Cathy Poole

Modern Women Writers
Series editor: **Maura Healy**

Longman

Acknowledgements

We are grateful to the following for permission to reproduce copyright material:

The author, Simon Banner, for an extract from his article on Anita Brookner in *The Guardian* 4.9.85 and BBC Enterprises Ltd for an extract from Inside Television published by Webb & Bower (1983).

Contents

Contents

Introduction

The novelist

It is always interesting to know a little about the writer of a novel. Anita Brookner was born in 1938 and now lives in London. She has devoted the whole of her working life to a successful career in the study and teaching of Fine Art, and in particular the study of French painting in the late eighteenth century. Her first novel was published in 1980. She has published six more since then.

Hotel du Lac first came out in 1984. Although in some ways it reads like a novel from an earlier time, the issues which it invites us to explore are very much those which concern us today.

The main character; the position of women in society

Edith Hope, the main character, earns her own living. She is a 'moderately successful' writer of romantic fiction. We follow her thoughts and feelings and find out about her life. Reading about her character and the difficulties she experiences helps us to think about the changing position of women in society. We find ourselves asking, along with Edith, what is acceptable behaviour for women today. She is told, 'You are a lady. They are rather out of fashion these days' (page 130). Certainly, in some ways, she is old fashioned. In other ways her behaviour is typical of a woman of her age, background and character who is responding to the pressures of the present time.

There have been many changes which have benefited women during this century. The suffragettes and the contribution of women to the 1914–18 war effort gained women the vote. The Women's Movement of the sixties helped to establish their right to equal pay and to recognition in their chosen field. Many women are now financially independent and achieve success in their careers. These improvements, however, do not necessarily bring with them happiness in women's personal lives.

A number of women feel confused. They have grown up with ideas from the past about how relationships should be. Yet the people they meet and the relationships they experience suggest new patterns of behaviour. Edith Hope's situation is typical. She is trapped between the old idea that a romantic suitor will ask your hand in marriage and that this will take care of everything, and the newer belief that women should make their own decisions about what they want from life and take steps to gain it. Edith can't allow herself to marry simply because she and other people think she ought to, nor is she able to accept life as it is, without marriage.

Edith is in many ways like the 'tortoise' heroines of the novels she writes, 'A mouse-like unassuming girl' (page 17). However, she is unlike them in that she does not 'get the hero while the scornful temptress with whom he had a stormy affair retreats baffled from the fray never to return' (page 17). Anita Brookner invites us to compare the behaviour of the 'tortoises', women like Edith, and 'hares', women like a character called Iris Pusey, who 'knew from the outset what some unfortunates never learn. She knew that the best is there to be taken, although there may not be enough to go round' (page 36). The suggestion is that Mrs Pusey knew what she wanted, how to get it and that you have move quickly in order to get what you want. Edith, who did not think in this way, could see the advantages of such an outlook.

Love, romance and marriage

Love, romance and male/female relationships are central to the novel. We are shown a number of different attitudes and experiences. For Edith, her lover was 'the breath of life' (page 143). This deeply romantic position is contrasted by the ideas of one of Edith's suitors. The advantage of marriage, as he sees it, is that it offers respectability. This respectability, he feels, gives the freedom to behave 'as badly as you like' (page 132). A further view is given by Iris Pusey, for whom early married life was 'like a dream' (page 27). Such a statement might sound romantic, were it not connected with the information that her late husband gave her everything she could wish for. She quotes his words: 'Iris, if it'll make you happy, buy it. I'll give you a blank cheque' (page 27). Through showing us these different views, Anita Brookner invites us to question the nature of love and romance. We are encouraged to consider carefully what ingredients make the ideal relationship.

The moral outlook of the book; changing values in our society

Our present-day thinking about morality is also affected by the conventions of the past. Now there are no clear rules in this area either. The teachings of the Church used to mould our thinking about morality. Nowadays, there are fewer regular church-goers than there used to be. If people do not go to church, and do not hear religious assemblies at school, then they are less likely to hold Christian values. For example, it used to be accepted that virtue is its own reward. Now this belief is being questioned. Edith Hope is again trapped between the old order and the new. She knows all about good behaviour. She also sees that those who behave as they wish, rather than as the old rules say they ought, appear to be happy and fulfilled.

There is no one character in the novel who represents the correct moral outlook. The writer shows us a range of different types of behaviour. She allows Edith and other characters to comment, but she leaves us to work out for ourselves what is the best way to behave. In this way the novel is typical of the present time. There are no rigid codes for behaviour and very few definite answers to moral questions.

Edith Hope's character; present-day thinking about writers

Anita Brookner's choice of heroine is also interesting. We live in an age when communications are better than ever before. Television cameras allow us to look more closely at public figures than was possible in any previous age. Perhaps partly because of this, we have developed an interest in their private lives. Details appear in newspaper daily. Anita Brookner pokes fun at this habit. Edith Hope is a writer of romantic fiction. As such she is of potential interest to her public, and so to us. However, Anita Brookner makes sure that she is not a glamorous character. She is quiet, ordinary, rather sad and not particularly successful in her assessment of the people she meets.

Over the last century there has been an increased interest in the personality of the artist. The feeling is that they see the world in a special way. Through the creation of Edith, Anita Brookner seems to be gently laughing at the belief that a novelist sees the world more clearly; Edith's concentration on fictional lives certainly does not give her increased speed in understanding people. In fact, she feels she perhaps needs an 'interpreter'. By her own description, she is 'preternaturally naive' (page 72).

The novel describes in detail a set of wealthy middle-class people. However, many of the issues raised by the novel are of equal interest to people from all areas of society. How should women of today behave? How much are our patterns of behaviour in relationships dictated by the habits of the past? Is it possible to change these? Does it matter how you treat other people? What is it that makes us happy? Should we worry about the feelings of others when seeking out our own happiness?

How the novel is written

The structure

Anita Brookner, like most writers of the 1980s, uses a straight-forward structure to tell her story. She shows us Edith Hope's existence over one month, the short period of her stay at Hotel du Lac. We are told what happens largely from Edith's point of view. For much of the novel, Anita Brookner reports what her main character is thinking: 'superstitiously she left the bulk of her clothes in her bag, signifying to herself that she could be off in a few minutes, if the chance arose, although knowing that everything would stay there and be hopelessly creased into the bargain' (page 5). Reading these details about the way her mind works help us to understand the kind of person she is.

Much of what we read is Edith's own memory of past events. As with all memories, these pass through Edith's mind in haphazard order. The time sequence shifts quickly into the past at particular points. For instance, Edith's admiration of a mother/daughter relationship which she observes at the hotel on a number of occasions prompts her to think about her relationship with her own mother during early childhood.

Anita Brookner begins the novel at the moment when Edith arrives at the Hotel du Lac. We are told that she has done 'an apparently dreadful thing' (page 2). We are then kept in suspense for another eight chapters before we are told the details. Our interest is sustained, however, by references to her wrong-doing and clues as to its nature. After we have been told about it, apart from a few references to past events in Edith's letters, all the action that occurs follows a chrono-logical sequence in the present.

Through this route, we reach what at first appears to be an unexpected ending. If we think about it, however, we, like Edith, realise how 'little surprised' (page 146) we are. Anita Brookner has carefully woven into the text certain clues which at first, do not seem significant – for example, the sound of a door closing at night. She has also created thoroughly consistent characters. If we think carefully about the type of people they are, then we realise that we could almost have predicted the outcome ourselves. This makes us realise that the ending of the novel is entirely realistic.

Creation of character and atmosphere

Like Jane Austen, Anita Brookner observes most closely the people in the society in which she lives, and presents us with a small group of them. She has a peculiar gift for characterisation. Her portraits are detailed, complete and often wickedly humorous. Our first sight of Monica, for instance, is of

> a tall woman of extraordinary slenderness and with the narrow nodding head of a grebe [who] rushed out of the bar, collapsed at the foot of the stairs, gathered the dog into her arms, covered it with kisses, and again, with the same boneless uncoiling movement, pressed the dog to her face like a cushion and returned to the bar. (page 8)

Notice the ways in which Anita Brookner makes Monica unusual. The choice of the word 'extraordinary' emphasises her slim figure. The metaphor which likens her to a grebe – a long-necked bird – adds to this impression as does the cleverly chosen phrase 'boneless uncoiling'. Study what we are told of Monica's treatment of her dog. Note the 'kisses' and the simile 'like a cushion' which is used to show the manner in which she holds the dog to her face. It is worth remembering that this is the first information we are given about Monica. The novelist, through her careful choice of words and phrases, has undoubtedly given us a clear picture of a rather intense, perhaps oversensitive, personality.

As for Edith, we experience her thoughts, read her letters

to David, hear her own version of her past, listen to the comments of Harold, Monica, Mr Neville, Penelope Milne and others about her. We see her behaviour in a variety of situations. Anita Brookner draws our attention to her figure, her cardigan, her shoes. We hear her conversations with a variety of different people. In this way, Anita Brookner makes her come to life and we are able to question her attitudes and her outlook with the feeling that we know her well.

The same kind of meticulous care is taken in the creation of atmosphere. Anita Brookner pays close attention to detail. Notice, for instance, the austere feeling which comes over in our first view of Edith's room in the hotel, and the way in which each item of the description and the words used to express it, help to build up this impression.

> ... She contemplated the room which was the colour of overcooked veal, veal coloured carpet and curtains, high narrow bed with veal coloured counterpane, small austere table with a correct chair placed tightly underneath it, a narrow costive wardrobe, and, at a very great height above her head, a tiny brass chandelier which, she knew, would eventually twinkle drearily with eight weak bulbs. Stiff white lace curtains, providing even more protection against the sparse daylight, could be parted to allow access. . . . (pages 2–3).

It is Anita Brookner's deft style and her detailed, witty, slightly cynical but careful observations of human behaviour which make this novel such an enjoyable one to read and to study.

Reading logs

Before you start reading

You will need a note book in which you can write down the thoughts which occur to you while you are reading the novel. These can be in note form. You will find it useful to look back at them when you are working on particular assignments, after reading the novel.

You should use your reading log for writing down all the notes and exercises which you are asked to do in the 'While you are reading' section. Most of these notes will only be seen by you, as you will use them for preparation work for your assignments later on. However, some of this work, such as the diary entry and the predicted ending, may be redrafted for a piece of coursework.

While you are reading

There is a range of activities here which take you through the text and help you focus on particular themes, characters and issues of importance. They will also help you to look at the way in which the novel is written; how Anita Brookner gives us clues about what is to happen, and how she creates character. Look briefly at these before you start to read the book. You will see that you are asked to stop at various points, in order to discuss what you have read so far, or to predict what is going to happen. Look carefully at these exercises now so that you will know when to stop reading.

The opening chapter

1 *Read carefully the first paragraph on page 1.*
   What kind of story will this be?

In a small group, *brainstorm* your ideas about what the plot will be for this story. This means that one person should quickly jot down everything that comes into the group's minds. It doesn't matter what order these thoughts are in; you can rearrange them and take out the ideas which don't work later.

Notice these phrases:

'all that could be seen was a receding area of grey'

'the vast grey lake, spreading like an anaesthetic'

'inhabitants, uncommunicative to begin with, were frequently rendered taciturn by the dense cloud that descended for days at a time'

'the gaunt remains of a thirteenth-century castle'

'the weather distressingly beyond control'

Could this be the beginning of
– a love story?
– a mystery story?
– a detective story?

2 *Read to the end of the chapter.*
   (a) The writer has kept us guessing about Edith Hope. Make short notes which you think might answer the following questions:
      (i) Why has she been 'banished' to this hotel 'by those who knew her best'? (page 12)
      (ii) Who is the David to whom she writes, and why is he important?

   (b) What kind of character is Edith Hope? In a pair or in small groups, talk about what you have gathered of her from this chapter.
      (i) Between you, think of *five* words or phrases which best seem to describe her.
      (ii) Look back over the chapter and pick out particular words and phrases from the book which you think prove your views.

(iii) Write the list of words on one side of the page and the quotation that goes with them on the other side, for example:

efficient   'a deliverer of typescripts well before the deadline' (page 2)

self-conscious   'I shall be ready to make the entrance' (page 5)

You have now learned how to select quotations. This will be useful for your written assignments after reading the book.

The hotel

1 *Reread the description of the Hotel du Lac and its surroundings on pages 1 and 6–8, and Edith's room on pages 2–3.*
   – Draw a rough sketch map of the area
   – Draw a rough plan or picture of Edith's room
   This will help you to focus on the kind of surroundings in which the novelist deliberately places Edith. The descriptions of the surroundings help to create the atmosphere.

2 *In pairs, act out the recommendation of this hotel by an ex-guest to another for whom it would be a suitable place to stay.*
   or
   Jot down in your journal a list of the kind of people who you think would go there.

Edith Hope

In the Introduction, I have talked about the way Anita Brookner prepares us for certain events, through the use of a series of clues.

1 (a) *Keep a page in your journal marked CLUES.*

List quotations and their page references which might help to build up a picture of Edith's life before she came to Geneva, and to tell you how it is that she came to the Hotel du Lac. Add your own suggestions, for example,

Clues	Comments
'to revert to what I was before I did that apparently dreadful thing' (page 2)	Edith has done something which others consider bad, but she doesn't.

(b) *When you have read up to the end of Chapter 8 (page 91), reread this page in your journal and the notes that you made after reading Chapter 1. Then write your own Chapter 9.*

Explain exactly what you think had happened to Edith, then read Anita Brookner's Chapter 9. Is it very different from your own piece? If so, in what ways?

Remember that Anita Brookner also gives us clues about the ending. You might like to jot down any information which you think might be a clue to the final outcome.

2 (a) *In a small group, prepare and read aloud the conversation between Edith and Harold Webb which occurs on pages 16–18, up to 'Thank you for lunch.'*

You will need:

    Edith ⎫ who should try to speak as though they
    Harold ⎭ really are the characters they represent.
    someone to read Harold's thoughts,
    Narrator's voice.

This will help you to focus on Edith Hope's ideas about relationships and the way she deals with them in her novels.

or

> (b) *Read pages 16–18 and make a short tape-recording of a talk which might have been given by Edith to others who have asked her to explain why she writes as she does.*

Edith as Vanessa Wilde

> 'The woman with the dog ... had not made the entrance that Edith had mentally written for her ...' (page 20)

Anita Brookner gives us frequent reminders that Edith Hope is a writer and suggests that this affects the way that she views the world.

1 *You have been asked to write a magazine article about the life and work of Vanessa Wilde. Make short notes in preparation for this.*
These should include:
   (i) the topics that she writes about;
   (ii) the titles which she has had published;
   (iii) her appearance and personality.
If you like, you can write the whole article when you have finished reading *Hotel du Lac*.

2 *Write a flow diagram to show the story of Edith Hope/Vanessa Wilde's latest novel.*
A flow diagram is a way of giving information through a series of headings which are connected by lines and arrows:

Other characters

The tall man in the light grey suit

He is first mentioned on page 39. Keep an account of all the times that

WHILE YOU ARE READING

we are told of his presence before we (and Edith) are properly intro-
duced, on page 54.

Before you reach that page, talk to a friend about him.

  (i) In what way might he be significant in this novel?

 (ii) What might his personality be like?

(iii) Why do you think that we are not, at first, told his name?

   When you have read to the end of the novel, look back over
these notes.

The Puseys

1 *Read to the end of Chapter 6.*

   (i) In what way do you think these people are important
       to Edith?

  (ii) In what ways are they important to the novel?

 (iii) Draw a flow chart showing how you think the novel will
       end. Do Edith and the Puseys leave the hotel at the
       same time?

2 *Read up to the end of page 111.*

Think carefully about what kind of person Jennifer is. 'Edith
had once or twice had the impression that behind her large
smiling face, Jennifer was somewhere else.' (page 25) If she
is 'somewhere else', what is she thinking about? What is her
attitude

    – to men?

    – to others in the hotel?

    – to her mother?

What does she want from life?

What kinds of words would she use when writing or talking?

   As Jennifer, write a diary entry for one or two evenings
spent at the Hotel du Lac. This will help you understand
the character Anita Brookner has created and how she has
done it.

xix

3 *In a group of two or three, improvise a shopping excursion for Iris and Jennifer Pusey.*

4 *Write a list of short quotations which give us an idea of what Iris Pusey is like.*

In the Introduction I have talked about ways in which Anita Brookner shows us what a character is like. Write a comment alongside each of your chosen quotations which explains what kind of technique is being used to present her to us. You may find the suggestions in the section (below) on David useful.

David

Look carefully at what we are told about David on pages 42–4, 64–7, 89, 96 and 104.

On one side of the page write a list of notes which say what you have learned about his character. On the opposite side of the page, write a note which explains which method Anita Brookner is using in order to create his personality. Here are some statements to help you.

- Anita Brookner allows his particular use of colloquialisms to give us a picture of a certain type of man.
- Anita Brookner chooses particular verbs with which to describe his actions.
- The way in which his physical appearance is described reflects his personality.
- Description of facial expressions suggests a certain type of person.
- Anita Brookner makes short statements about his behaviour which help us to sum up his personality.
- We are told what he is thinking; this allows us to make judgements about him.
- We are given accounts of certain habits which are peculiar to him and therefore help us to know what kind of person he is.

- Other characters' reactions to David give us a different point of view.
- Use of simile, for example 'sheep-like expression', to describe Edith makes the picture of a character clearer in our minds.
- Use of contrast with other characters makes it clearer what he is like.

Alain

Act out the conversation which might have taken place between Alain and Maryvonne after they had left the Puseys' room (page 109).

Romance

The word 'romantic' is used several times in this novel. Look carefully at these definitions of 'romance' and 'romantic' from the *Longman Dictionary of Contemporary English*.

ro·mance¹ /rəʊˈmæns, rə-/ *n* **1** [C] a story of love, adventure, strange happenings, etc., often set in a distant time or place, whose events are happier or grander or more exciting than those of real life: *a romance about a king who married a beggar girl* **2** [U] the quality that such stories have; the quality in the human mind that hopes for such experiences in real life: *the romance of life in the Wild West* **3** [C] a love affair: *How is your little romance with Julia going?*

romance² *v* [I∅] **1** [(*about*)] to tell improbable stories or ROMANCEs¹ (1): *Is he telling the truth or romancing about his famous relations?* **2** [(*with*)] to carry on a love affair

ro·man·tic¹ /rəʊˈmæntɪk, rə-/ *adj* **1** [B] belonging to or suggesting ROMANCE¹ (1): *a very romantic love story* **2** [B] *sometimes derog* fanciful; not practical; showing (too much) liking for dreams of love, adventure, etc.: *She has romantic ideas about becoming a famous actress* **3** [Wa5;A;(B)] (*often cap.*) marked by ROMANTICISM: *romantic poetry* —**~ally** *adv* [Wa4]

romantic² *n* **1** a ROMANTIC¹ (2) person: *He was a romantic who went off to the South Seas to paint pictures* **2** (*often cap.*) a writer, painter, etc., whose work shows ROMANTICISM

ro·man·ti·cis·m /rəʊˈmænt₁sɪzəm, rə-/ n [U] (*often cap.*) (in art and literature) the quality of admiring feeling rather than thought, and wild beauty rather than things made by man —compare REALISM, CLASSICISM — **-cist** n

ro·man·ti·cize, -cise /rəʊˈmænt₁saɪz, rə-/ v [I∅;T1] *derog* to tell improbable and ROMANTIC¹ (2) stories (about); make (an event) sound more ROMANTIC by adding interesting or exciting details: *Just keep to the facts and stop romanticizing!*

Using your own words if possible, write down the meaning which best suits the word as (i) Mrs Pusey and (ii) Mr Neville, use it.

Predicting the story

1 *On a number of occasions, Edith thought that she heard a door close. Make a note of these occasions and try to guess the significance of the noise.*

2 *Read up to the end of Chapter 11.*
With a friend, discuss what you think Edith said to Mr Neville after she had 'thought about it'.
In a small group, debate what her decision ought to be. Remember always to give a reason for your opinion.

As soon as you have finished the novel

1 Jot down all the questions which are still in your mind about the characters. Show them to a friend; between you, try to find some answers.

2 In her final letter to David, Edith writes: 'This is the last letter I shall write to you and the first one that I shall ever post' (page 142). Write notes saying what you think is the importance of this statement in the novel as a whole. Remember to mention:

- Edith's 'subterranean' level of existence (page 70)
- Edith's relationships with men
- her place in David's life, his place in hers
- Anita Brookner's method of drawing our attention to particular aspects of character through keeping the reader waiting
- the fact that the letter is never sent.

3 Do you like the ending? Had you imagined a different ending? Write the ending you would have chosen for the novel.

or

Write the chapter which you imagine to take place after Edith has sent the telegram. When you have written it, swop with someone else who has completed this piece. Write comments on each other's work.

- Do the characters behave as you would expect them to?
- Does the new chapter reflect the mood of the novel?
- In what ways do descriptions of the setting add to the atmosphere of the story?
- Think of more comments of your own.

Hotel du Lac

For Rosamond Lehmann

1

From the window all that could be seen was a receding area of grey. It was to be supposed that beyond the grey garden, which seemed to sprout nothing but the stiffish leaves of some unfamiliar plant, lay the vast grey lake, spreading like an anaesthetic towards the invisible further shore, and beyond that, in imagination only, yet verified by the brochure, the peak of the Dent d'Oche, on which snow might already be slightly and silently falling. For it was late September, out of season; the tourists had gone, the rates were reduced, and there were few inducements for visitors in this small town at the water's edge, whose inhabitants, uncommunicative to begin with, were frequently rendered taciturn by the dense cloud that descended for days at a time and then vanished without warning to reveal a new landscape, full of colour and incident: boats skimming on the lake, passengers at the landing stage, an open air market, the outline of the gaunt remains of a thirteenth-century castle, seams of white on the far mountains, and on the cheerful uplands to the south a rising backdrop of apple trees, the fruit sparkling with emblematic significance. For this was a land of prudently harvested plenty, a land which had conquered human accidents, leaving only the weather distressingly beyond control.

Edith Hope, a writer of romantic fiction under a more thrusting name, remained standing at the window, as if an access of good will could pierce the mysterious opacity with which she had been presented, although she had been promised a tonic cheerfulness, a climate devoid of illusions, an utterly commonsensical, not to say pragmatic, set of circumstances – quiet hotel, excellent cuisine, long walks, lack of excitement, early nights – in which she could be counted upon to retrieve her serious and hard-working personality and to forget the unfortunate lapse which had led to this brief exile, in this apparently unpopulated place, at this slowly darkening time of the year, when she should have been at home . . . But it was home, or, rather, 'home', which had become inimical all at once, so that she had acquiesced, rather frightened at what was happening to her, when her friends had uggested a short break, and had allowed herself to be driven to the airport by her friend and neighbour, Penelope Milne, who, tight-lipped, was prepared to forgive her only on condition that she disappeared for a decent length of time and came back older, wiser, and properly apologetic. For I am not to be allowed my lapse, as if I were an artless girl, she thought; and why should I be? I am a serious woman who should know better and am judged by my friends to be past the age of indiscretion; several people have remarked upon my physical resemblance to Virginia Woolf; I am a householder, a rate-payer, a good plain cook, and a deliverer of typescripts well before the deadline; I sign anything that is put in front of me; I never telephone my publisher; and I make no claims for my particular sort of writing, although I understand that it is doing quite well. I have held this rather dim and trusting personality together for a considerable length of time, and although I have certainly bored others I was not to be allowed to bore myself. My profile was deemed to be low and it was agreed by those who thought they knew me that it should stay that way. And no doubt after a curative stay in this grey solitude (and I notice that the leaves of that plant are quite immobile) I shall be allowed back, to resume my peaceable existence, and to revert to what I was before I did that apparently dreadful thing, although, frankly, once I had done it I didn't give it another thought. But I do now. Yes.

Turning her back on the toneless expanse beyond the window, she contemplated the room, which was the colour of over-cooked veal: veal-coloured carpet and curtains, high, narrow bed with veal-coloured counterpane, small austere table with a correct chair placed tightly underneath it, a narrow, costive wardrobe, and, at a very great height above her head, a tiny brass chandelier, which, she knew, would eventually twinkle drearily with eight weak bulbs. Stiff white lace curtains, providing even more protection against the sparse daylight, could be parted to allow access, through long windows, to a narrow strip of balcony on which were placed a green metal table and chair. I shall be able to write there when the weather is fine, she thought, and moved to her bag to extract two long folders, one of which contained the first chapter of *Beneath the Visiting Moon*, on which she planned to work calmly throughout this curious hiatus in her life. But it was to the other folder that her hands went and, on opening it, she moved instinctively to the table and was soon seated on the unyielding chair, her pen uncapped, her surroundings ignored.

'My dearest David (she wrote),

'A cold coming I had of it. Penelope drove fast and kept her eyes grimly ahead, as if escorting a prisoner from the dock to a maximum security wing. I was disposed to talk – it is not every day that I get on an aeroplane and the pills I had got from the doctor had the effect of making me rather loquacious – but my intervention did not seem to be too welcome. Anyway, she relented once we were at Heathrow and found me a trolley for my bag and told me where I could get a cup of coffee, and suddenly she was gone and I felt terrible, not sad but light-headed and rather entertaining and with no one to talk to. I drank my coffee and paced around and tried to absorb all the details, as people think writers do (except you, my darling, who never think about it at all) and suddenly I caught sight of myself in the glass in the Ladies and saw my extremely correct appearance and thought, I should not be here! I am out of place! Milling crowds, children crying, everyone intent on being somewhere else, and here was this mild-looking, slightly bony woman in a long cardigan, distant, inoffensive, quite nice eyes, rather large hands and feet, meek neck, not wanting to go anywhere, but having given my word that I would stay away for a month until everyone decides that I am myself again. For a moment I panicked, for I am myself

3

now, and was then, although this fact was not recognized. Not drowning, but waving.

'Anyway, I got over that, though it was not easy, and joined the most reliable set of people I could find, knowing, without bothering to ask, that they were bound to be going to Switzerland, and very soon I was on the plane and a quite charming man sat next to me and told me about this conference he was attending in Geneva. I deduced that he was a doctor; in fact, I had him down as a specialist in tropical diseases, particularly as he told me that he did most of his work in Sierra Leone, but it turned out that he had something to do with tungsten. So much for the novelist's famed powers of imagination. Nevertheless I felt a bit better, and he told me about his wife and daughters and how he was flying back to them in two days' time to have a weekend at home before he goes back to Sierra Leone. And within an extraordinarily short time we were there (I notice that I say "there" and not "here") and he put me in a taxi, and after about half an hour I ended up here (and it is beginning to be "here" rather than "there") and very soon I shall have to unpack and wash and tidy my hair and go downstairs and try to find a cup of tea.

'The place seems to be deserted. I noticed only one elderly woman as I came in, very small, with a face like a bulldog, and legs so bowed that she seemed to throw herself from side to side in her effort to get ahead, but doing so with such grim conviction that I instinctively got out of the way. She walked with a stick and wore one of those net veils on her head covered with small blue velvet bows. I had her down as a Belgian confectioner's widow, but the boy carrying my bags nodded vestigially and murmured "Madame la Comtesse" as she rocked past. So much for the novelist's famed powers, etc. In any event I was processed so speedily into this room (almost induced into it) that I couldn't take in anything else. It seems quiet, warm, fairly spacious. The weather might, I suppose, be described as calm.

'I think about you all the time. I try to work out where you are, but this is rather difficult, surrounded as I am by the time change, minimal though it is, and the lingering effects of my pills, and all these sad cypresses. In a manner of speaking. But tomorrow is Friday, and when it begins to get dark I shall be able to imagine you getting in the car and driving to the cottage. And then, of course, the weekend, about which I try not to think. You cannot know . . .'

At this point she put down her pen and massaged her eyes briefly, sitting for a moment with her elbows on the table and her head bent into her hands. Then, blinking, she took up her pen again and continued her letter.

'Ridiculous to tell you to take care of yourself, because you never think of all the mild precautions that others take, and in any case there is nothing I can do to make you. My dear life, as my father used to call my mother, I miss you so much.'

She remained seated at the table for a few minutes, then took a long breath, and put the cap back on her pen. Tea, she thought. I need tea. And then a walk, a very long walk along the lake shore, and then a bath, and change into my blue dress, and by that time I shall be ready to make the entrance, always so difficult to negotiate, into the dining room. And then there is all the business of the meal to get through, which will take a bit of time, and after that I shall sit around and talk to someone, it hardly matters to whom, if only to the bulldog lady. And I need an early night, so that won't be too bad. In fact I am quite tired already. She yawned until her eyes watered, and then stood up.

Unpacking took a few minutes. Superstitiously, she left the bulk of her clothes in her bag, signifying to herself that she could be off in a few minutes if the chance arose, although knowing that everything would stay there and be hopelessly creased into the bargain. It had ceased to matter. Her hair-brush and nightgown were carried into the bathroom. She surveyed her appearance, which seemed to be no different, and then, retrieving bag and key, she stepped out into a corridor vibrant with absence. A pale light filtered through a large window over the landing. The walls seemed to enshrine a distant memory of substantial meals. There was nobody about, although through a door further along the corridor she could hear the faint sound of a radio.

The Hotel du Lac (Famille Huber) was a stolid and digni-fied building, a house of repute, a traditional establishment, used to welcoming the prudent, the well-to-do, the retired, the self-effacing, the respected patrons of an earlier era of tourism. It had made little effort to smarten itself up for the passing trade which it had always despised. Its furnishings, although austere, were of excellent quality, its linen spotless, its service impeccable. Its reputation among knowledgeable professionals attracted apprentices of good character who had a serious interest in the hotel trade, but this was the only concession it made to a recognition of its own resources. As far as guests were concerned, it took a perverse pride in its very absence of attractions, so that any visitor mildly looking for a room would be puzzled and deflected by the sparseness of the terrace, the muted hush of the lobby, the absence of piped music, public telephones, advertisements for scenic guided tours, or notice boards directing one to the amenities of the town. There was no sauna, no hairdresser, and certainly no glass cases displaying items of jewellery; the bar was small and dark, and its austerity did not encourage people to linger. It was implied that prolonged drinking, whether for purposes of business or as a personal indulgence, was not *comme il faut*, and if thought absolutely necessary should be conducted either in the privacy of one's suite or in the more popular establishments where such leanings were not unknown. Chambermaids were rarely encountered after ten o'clock in the morning, by which time all household noises had to be silenced; no vacuuming was heard, no carts of dirty linen were glimpsed, after that time. A discreet rustle announced the reappearance of the maids to turn down the beds and tidy the rooms once the guests had finished changing to go down to dinner. The only publicity from which the hotel could not distance itself was the word of mouth recommendations of patrons of long standing.

What it had to offer was a mild form of sanctuary, an assurance of privacy, and the protection and the discretion that attach themselves to blamelessness. This last quality being less than attractive to a surprising number of people, the Hotel du Lac was usually half empty, and at this time of the year, at the end of the season, was resigned to catering for a mere handful of guests before closing its doors for the winter. The few visitors who were left from the modest number who had taken their decorous holiday in the high summer months were, however, treated with the same courtesy and deference as if they were treasured patrons of long standing, which, in some cases, they were. Naturally, no attempt was made to entertain them. Their needs were provided for and their characters perused with equal care. It was assumed that they would live up to the hotel's standards, just as the hotel would live up to theirs. And if any problems were encountered, those problems would be dealt with discreetly. In this way the hotel was known as a place which was unlikely to attract unfavourable attention, a place guaranteed to provide a restorative sojourn for those whom life had mistreated or merely fatigued. Its name and situation figured in the card indexes of those whose business it is to know such things. Certain doctors knew it, many solicitors knew it, brokers and accountants knew it. Travel agents did not know it, or had forgotten it. Those families who benefit from the periodic absence of one of their more troublesome members treasured it. And the word got round.

And of course it was an excellent hotel. And its situation on the lake was agreeable. The climate was not brilliant, but in comparison with other, similar, resorts, it was equable. The resources of the little town were not extensive, but cars could be hired, excursions could be taken, and the walking was pleasant if unexciting. The scenery, the view, the mountain, were curiously unemphatic, as if delineated in the water-colours of an earlier period. While the young of all nations

7

hurtled off to the sun and the beaches, jamming the roads and the airports, the Hotel du Lac took a quiet pride, and sometimes it was very quiet indeed, in its isolation from the herd, knowing that it had a place in the memory of its old friends, knowing too that it would never refuse a reasonable request from a new client, provided that the new client had the sort of unwritten references required from an hotel of this distinction, and that the request had come from someone whose name was already on the Huber family's files, most of which went back to the beginning of the century.

As she descended the wide, shallow stairs Edith could hear well-behaved laughter echoing from some sort of salon where she supposed tea to be in progress, and then, as she approached, as if drawn to this sound, a sudden furious barking, high-pitched, peevish, boding ill for future peace. At the foot of the stairs crouched a very small dog, quivering with anxiety, its eyes covered by its hair. When no one came to see what was wrong, it started up again at full volume, but experimentally, like a baby. A prolonged keening, as if it were undergoing unimaginable torture, brought cries of 'Kiki! Kiki! Naughty dog!', and a tall woman, of extraordinary slenderness, and with the narrow nodding head of a grebe, rushed out of the bar, collapsed at the foot of the stairs, gathered the dog into her arms, covered it with kisses, and again, with the same boneless uncoiling movement, pressed the dog to her face like a cushion, and returned to the bar. A puddle on the last step brought a momentary closing of the eyes and a quick snap of the fingers from the manager. As a boy in a white jacket wielded a cloth, impassively, as if this happened fairly often, the manager of the Hotel du Lac (Famille Huber) indicated to Edith Hope his distress that this incident should mar her arrival, and at the same time expressed dissociation from the misdemeanours of animals and, more important, from those unwise enough to harbour them. For the latter he would, of course, provide shelter, but shelter without complicity.

How interesting, thought Edith. That woman was English.

And such an extraordinary shape. Probably a dancer. And she promised herself to think about this later.

The salon was more agreeable than her room would have led her to expect, furnished with a deep blue carpet, many round glass tables, comfortably traditional armchairs, and a small upright piano at which an elderly man with a made-up bow tie was playing mild selections from post-war musicals. With tea inside her, and a slice of excellent cherry cake, Edith plucked up the courage to look around. The room was sparsely populated; she supposed that most people would only come back for dinner. The pug-faced lady was eating grimly, her legs wide apart, crumbs falling unnoticed on to her lap. Two shadowy men were whispering in a far corner. A greyish couple, man and wife or brother and sister, were checking their air tickets, and the man, who had by no means finished his tea, was sent off periodically to see if the car had arrived. Although the room was bright and cheerful, its most notable feature was its air of deadly calm. Edith, recognizing the fate to which she had been consigned, sighed, but reminded herself that this was an excellent opportunity to finish *Beneath the Visiting Moon*, although it was not an opportunity that she herself had sought.

When she next raised her eyes from her book – a book from which she had absorbed not a single word – it was to find an unexpected note of glamour in the person of a lady of indeterminate age, her hair radiantly ash blonde, her nails scarlet, her dress a charming (and expensive) printed silk, beating time to the music with her hand, a smile of pleasure on her pretty face, while the waitresses, obviously attracted to such a positive presence, hovered round her, offering more cake, more tea. She bestowed a warm smile on them, and an even warmer one on the elderly pianist, who, when he got up and folded his music, came over to her and murmured something which made her laugh, then kissed her hand and left, his stiff, narrow back radiant with the appreciation he had received. Leaning back in her chair, her cup and saucer raised to her chin, this lady drank her tea with some delicacy, even with a sense of favourable presentation, and she did indeed make a delightful spectacle, devoid as she was of the anguish that attacks some people in strange places, and clearly at home in the ambience of the hotel, even if it was three quarters empty.

Edith watched her as if under hypnosis, sorry to have missed a moment of this spectacle. Rings sparkled on the hand that brought a delicate lace handkerchief to her lips. When her tray had been taken away, Edith waited keenly to see what she would do with the hiatus between tea and dinner, so dispiriting to the unexpected or unaccompanied hotel guest. But of course this lady was not alone. 'Here I am,' carolled a young voice, and into the salon came a girl wearing rather tight white trousers (rather too tight, thought Edith) which outlined a bottom shaped like a large Victoria plum, 'There you are, darling,' cried the lady, who was, who must be, her mother. 'I've just finished. Have you had tea?'

'No, but it doesn't matter,' said the girl, who was, Edith saw, a rather paler version of her mother, or rather the same model as her mother but not brought to the same state of high finish.

'But my darling!' exclaimed the older lady. 'You must have tea! You must be exhausted! Just ring the bell. They can make some more.'

As one of the waitresses approached, they both turned on her a winning smile, begged for tea, but with an assurance that it would certainly be forthcoming, and immediately, and then lapsed into an engrossing conversation of which Edith could only hear the odd word, together with the joyous and congratulatory spasms of laughter that escaped them both from time to time. When the second tray arrived, they both turned their smiling faces to the waitress, thanked her effusively, and resumed their dialogue, although the girl lingered, as if her part in the ritual might just conceivably be prolonged, but, 'That will be all, dear,' said the lady in the silk dress, and settled down to contemplation of her daughter.

The daughter must be about twenty-five, thought Edith, unmarried, but not worried about it. 'She's in no hurry,' she could imagine the mother saying, with her fine smile. 'She's quite happy as she is.' And the daughter would blush and bridle, thus inviting lubricious speculation on the part of the elderly gentlemen who would, Edith was sure, be in relatively constant attendance on the mother. I must stop this, she said to herself. I do not have to make up their lives for them. They are in fact doing very nicely without me. And she felt a pang of wistfulness for such a mother, so good-humoured, so elegantly turned out, so insistent that her daughter should have tea, although it was nearly six o'clock. She felt a pang of wistfulness too for the daughter, so confident, so at ease with what was provided for her ... And they were English, although not of a type with which she was familiar, and rather well-off, and having a good time. They looked as though they always did.

At last they decided to make a move, and when the mother made two attempts to lever herself out of her chair, her daughter hovering energetically beside her, as if knowing exactly when to intervene, Edith saw with some surprise that the older lady was in fact rather stiff in the joints, and that the shining impression of fairly youthful maturity, so impressive from a distance, was not prolonged when she stood up. Thoughtfully, she adjusted their ages, which she had put in the upper fifties and the middle twenties, to the upper sixties and the early thirties. But the appearance was excellent, in both cases. And she was secretly very pleased when the older lady, opposite whom she had been seated, but at some distance, turned round and gave her a mild smile of acknowledgment before she left the room.

Then there was nothing to do but go for a walk.

Through the silent garden, through an iron gate, across the busy road, and along the shore of the lake she walked in the fading light of that grey day. The silence engulfed her once she was past the town's one intersection, and it seemed as if she

11

might walk for ever, uninterrupted, with only her thoughts for company. This solitude to which she had been banished, by those who knew best, was not what she had had in mind. And this dim, veiled, discreet, but unfriendly weather: was this to be an additional accompaniment to this time of trial, for someone who had rashly travelled without a heavy coat? The lake was utterly still; a solitary lamp gleamed above her, turning the limp leaves of a plane tree to brilliant emerald. There is no need for me to stay here if I don't want to, she decided. Nobody is actually forcing me. But I must give it a try, if only to make things easier when I get home. The place is not totally unpopulated. I do need a rest. I could perhaps give it a week. And there is a lot to find out, for someone of my benighted persuasion, although of course none of those people would fit into the sort of fiction I write. But that very long, narrow woman, that beautiful woman, with the tiresome dog. And more than that, the glamorous pair who seem so at ease here. Why are they here? But women, women, only women, and I do so love the conversation of men. Oh David, David, she thought.

Her walk along the lake shore reminded her of nothing so much as those silent walks one takes in dreams, and in which unreason and inevitability go hand in hand. As in dreams she felt both despair and a sort of doomed curiosity, as if she must pursue this path until its purpose were revealed to her. The cast of her mind on this evening, and the aspect of the path itself, seemed to promise an unfavourable outcome: shock, betrayal, or at the very least a train missed, an important occasion attended in rags, an appearance in the dock on an unknown charge. The light, too, was that of dreams, an uncertain penumbra surrounding this odd pilgrimage, neither day nor night. In the real world through which she walked she was aware of certain physical characteristics: a perfectly straightforward gravel path flanked by two rows of trees standing in beaten earth, on one side the lake, invisible now, on the other, presumably, the town, but a town so small and so well ordered that one would never hear the screaming of brakes or the hooting of horns or the noise of voices raised in extravagant farewell. Only the modest sound of a peaceable file of evening traffic going home came faintly to her ears from somewhere beyond the trees, out of sight. Much louder was the sound of her own steps on the gravel, so loud that it seemed intrusive, and after a while she began to walk on the soft earth of the path nearest the lake. Beneath the light of an occasional lamp, she walked on uninterrupted, as if she were the only one abroad in this silent place. A perceptible chill rose from the water, which she could no longer see, and she shivered in her long cardigan. Doomed for a certain time to walk the earth, she thought, and, brooding but acquiescent, she carried on until she thought it time to be allowed to stop. Then she turned and retraced her steps.

Walking back through the twilight she saw the hotel from afar, lit up, falsely festive. I must make an effort, she decided, although she knew that a different sort of woman would have said, with a worldly sigh, 'I suppose I must put in an appearance.'

In the silent foyer, bright lights, a mumble from the television room, and a smell of meat. She went up to change.

At the desk, M. Huber the elder, retired but still active, benevolent and only mildly intrusive, was enjoying his favourite moment of the day. He opened the register to see who had gone and who had arrived. Business was of course very slack at this time of the year; the place was bound to be half empty in the month before the winter closure. The German family had gone, he noted; the noise of their going had indeed penetrated to his sitting room on the fifth floor. That curious elderly couple from the Channel Islands had left after tea. The conference at Geneva might yield the odd visitor, someone who decided to stay on, perhaps, and go back after the weekend. Otherwise, only the regulars were left: the Comtesse de Bonneuil, Mme Pusey and her daughter, the woman with the dog whom he refused to name, although her husband was in the English Gotha, and as to whom his son-in-law had received certain instructions. One new arrival. Hope, Edith Johanna. An unusual name for an English lady. Perhaps not entirely English. Perhaps not entirely a lady. Recommended, of course. But in this business one never knew.

2

Dressed for dinner, in her Liberty silk smock, her long narrow feet tamed into plain kid pumps, Edith sought for ways of delaying the moment at which she would be forced to descend into the dining room and take her first meal in public. She even wrote a few paragraphs of *Beneath the Visiting Moon*, then on re-reading them, realized that she had used the same device in *The Stone and the Star*, and crossed them out. And in crossing them out, understood exactly where she would have to go when she started again. Thus slightly reassured, with tomorrow's work tentatively programmed, she closed the folder, took up her bag and her key, and walked resolutely out of the room.

From the same not too distant point along the corridor she could hear the radio again, and also bath water, and as she went towards the stairs there seemed to be a sudden emanation of a rosy scent, signalling the sort of preparation made by someone with a proper sense of her own presence. The woman with the dog, thought Edith. She will emerge, rather late, in some stunning creation, flat-stomached and disdainful, the dog under her arm. I must try and talk to her. There will, she thought painfully, be nothing else to do after dinner.

Downstairs all was deserted, and she realized that she was too early. The only sounds came from the bar, where subdued masculine conversation, unbroken by laughter or conviviality, was in progress. She would have liked a gin and tonic but could not quite make the effort. She sat down at a small table in the salon and picked up a crumpled copy of the *Gazette de Lausanne* which someone had left. Curious that it had not been cleared away, she thought; the house-keeping here seems so very careful. But at that moment the bulldog-faced lady, whom she must remember to address properly, if she were ever called upon to address her at all, appeared in the doorway, wearing an all-purpose black dress and having changed her blue veil with the bows for a black one with a few slightly precarious sequins, raised her stick and said, 'Ah!' Edith held up the *Gazette de Lausanne* with an enquiring smile. Mme de Bonneuil nodded and began rocking her way through the thicket of unoccupied chairs and tables. Edith rose to meet her, but Mme de Bonneuil made surprisingly rapid progress, and Edith was stalled at the next table but two. '*Merci*,' said Mme de Bonneuil, raising her stick again. '*Je vous en prie*,' said Edith, and returned to her chair. They were the first words she had spoken since her arrival.

Leaning back and closing her eyes briefly, she allowed her dread of the evening before her to come to the surface. In any event, meals in public were not to her taste, even when she was accompanied. She remembered with a slight shudder the last meal she had had before leaving England. Her agent, Harold Webb, had taken her out to lunch. He had clearly meant to raise her spirits, had assured her of his confidence in her, had even told her that he intended to negotiate a higher advance for her next book. 'This other business will blow over,' he had said, lighting an unaccustomed cigar. A mild and scholarly man who looked like a country doctor, he disliked the more sociable aspects of his calling, but had nevertheless booked a table in a cathedral-like restaurant, where the patrons cowered in worship before the marvels to be set in front of them, and had gamely tackled the intricately coiled fillet of fish which had seemed to be the simplest item on the menu. Edith, regretting the Perrier water which always gave her wind, stared moodily into the distance. Conversation was not easy.

'I like the idea of the new one,' said Harold, after a longish pause. 'Although I have to tell you that the romantic market is beginning to change. It's sex for the young woman executive now, the *Cosmopolitan* reader, the girl with the executive briefcase.'

Receiving no response, he made play with the tiny fan of fretted carrot placed on a side plate and, having dealt with that, returned to the attack.

'What does she take with her on that business trip to Brussels?'

'Glasgow,' emended Edith.

'What? Oh, well, probably. But anyway, she wants something to reassure her that being liberated is fun. She wants something to flatter her ego when she's spending a lonely night in an hotel. She wants something to reflect her lifestyle.'

'Harold,' said Edith, 'I simply do not know anyone who has a lifestyle. What does it mean? It implies that everything you own was bought at exactly the same time, about five years ago, at the most. And anyway, if she's all that liberated, why doesn't she go down to the bar and pick someone up? I'm sure it's entirely possible. It's just that most women don't do it. And why don't they do it?' she asked, with a sudden return of assurance. 'It's because they prefer the old myths, when it comes to the crunch. They want to believe that they are going to be discovered, looking their best, behind closed doors, just when they thought that all was lost, by a man who has battled across continents, abandoning whatever he may have had in his in-tray, to reclaim them. Ah! If only it were true,' she said, breathing hard, and spearing a slice of kiwi fruit which remained suspended on her fork as she bent her head and thought this one out. She really does look remarkably Bloomsburian, thought Harold, viewing the hollowed cheeks and the pursed lips.

'Well, my dear, you know best,' he said, not wishing to upset her more than she had already been upset by that other business. 'I just thought that . . .'

'And what is the most potent myth of all?' she went on, in the slightly ringing tones that caused him to make a discreet sign to the waiter for the bill. 'The tortoise and the hare,' she pronounced. 'People love this one, especially women. Now you will notice, Harold, that in my books it is the mouse-like unassuming girl who gets the hero, while the scornful temptress with whom he has had a stormy affair retreats baffled from the fray, never to return. The tortoise wins every time.

This is a lie, of course,' she said, pleasantly, but with auth-ority, the kiwi fruit slipping back unnoticed onto her plate. 'In real life, of course, it is the hare who wins. Every time. Look around you. And in any case it is my contention that Aesop was writing for the tortoise market. Axiomatically,' she cried, her voice rising with enthusiasm. 'Hares have no time to read. They are too busy winning the game. The propaganda goes all the other way, but only because it is the tortoise who is in need of consolation. Like the meek who are going to inherit the earth,' she added, with a brief smile. After a pause, she addressed herself to what was left on her plate, ate it in one dismissive mouthful, and leaned back, still lost in her argument.

He reflected that she was not a professor's daughter for nothing, but that she could be relied upon to get back to work fairly soon, and that, after a break, she would probably come up with yet another modest but substantial seller.

'Of course,' said Edith, ladling chips of sugar coloured liked bath salts into her coffee, 'you could argue that the hare might be affected by the tortoise lobby's propaganda, might become more prudent, circumspect, slower, in fact. But the hare is always convinced of his own superiority; he simply does not recognize the tortoise as a worthy adversary. That is why the hare wins,' she concluded. 'In life, I mean. Never in fiction. At least, not in mine. The facts of life are too terrible to go into my kind of fiction. And my readers certainly do not want them there. You see, Harold, my readers are essentially virtuous. And as far as they are concerned – as far as *I* am concerned – those multi-orgasmic girls with the executive brief-cases can go elsewhere. They will be adequately catered for. There are hucksters in every market place.'

'I see you are getting back your old form,' said Harold, counting out a quantity of notes.

'Thank you for lunch, Harold,' Edith said, in the busy street outside. The coming separation from his kindly and self-effacing concern struck her more forcibly now than it had done hitherto. He was the only person who could be trusted to get in touch with her once she had gone away. He was the only person – well, almost – who knew where she was going. He was, alas, not the only person who knew why she was going. She looked imploringly into his eyes, aware that he had paid far too much money for a meal that would leave him hungry in an hour's time. Her own appetite was gone, quite gone. It hardly mattered what she ate these days, since she no longer mattered to herself. But those lovely meals that she had cooked for David, those heroic fry-ups, those blow-outs that he always seemed to require when they eventually got out of bed, at such awkward times, after midnight, sometimes, leaving it till the last minute before he raced back to Holland Park through the silent streets. 'I never get this stuff at home,' he would say lovingly, spearing a chip and inserting it into the yolk of a fried egg. Anxious, in her nightgown, she would watch him, a saucepan of baked beans to hand. Judging the state of his appetite with the eye of an expert, she would take another dish and ladle on to his plate a quivering mound of egg custard. 'Food fit for heroes,' he would sigh contentedly, his lean milky body forever resistant to the fattening effects of such a diet. 'Smashing,' he would pronounce, leaning back, replete. 'Any tea going?' But even as he drank his tea she would notice him quickening, straightening, becoming more rapid and decisive in his movements, and when he passed his hands over his short, dark red hair she would know that the transition was in progress and that he would soon get dressed. Then, she felt, she knew him less. All the business of cuff-links and watches belonged to his other life; this was what he did every morning while his wife called to the children who were going to be late. And finally she felt she hardly knew him at all, although she watched from behind the curtain as he ran out to the car, hasty now, and roared off into the night. It always felt as if he had gone for ever. But he had always come back. Sooner or later, he had come back.

It had seemed to her that the daylight hours were spent

simply waiting for him. And yet there were five novels, of some length, there to prove that she had not spent her time gazing out of the window, like the Lady of Shalott. It was, she recognized, a tortoise existence, despite the industry. That was why she wrote for tortoises, like herself.

But now I am reduced to pure tortoisedom, she thought, opening her eyes and gazing fearfully around the still deserted salon. But the appearance of a waiter in the doorway, with a napkin over his arm, gave her an access of determination, if only to get the meal over, for now she wanted to be alone, in her room, so as to think. Those pills must have worn off, she thought, feeling rather dizzy as she stood up, her throat aching with suppressed yawns. This is when character tells, as Father would say. And she urged herself onward to the dining room, prepared to eat because it was good for her, and to remain in an equable frame of mind for as long as possible.

The dining room was in fact very pleasant, with its long windows overlooking the garden, now quite black, and the small bunches of rather homely flowers on each spotless white tablecloth. It was also deserted. A table in the corner was occupied by four men in grey suits who kept up the same absorbed monotone that she had already located in the bar. Mme de Bonneuil, chewing steadily and without expression, had a curious way of taking her wine, in large gulps, as if rinsing her mouth out, and between courses would sit with her hands on the table, waiting for more. Edith could just see, embedded in her brownish fingers, small rings, one crested, but with the indentations worn away. The woman with the dog, a crêpe de Chine blouse hanging rather gauntly from her long neck and narrow shoulders, proved to be something of a disappointment, for she had not made the entrance that Edith had mentally written for her and was hunched in her seat, rather dishevelled about the hair, at an adjacent table, the impassive boy in the white jacket standing like a footman behind her chair. Kiki snuffled beside her, and was picked up from time to time and pressed to his mistress's face, a face,

Edith noted, which now gave minute hints of ultimate disintegration. With Kiki now on her lap, the woman's wavering fork, used more for flourishing than for eating, contrived to create an impression of food being consumed, although Edith could see quite a lot of it sliding down towards the tablecloth; somehow it never quite fell, for Kiki would jump up and retrieve it, rather like a trained seal. Edith had the impression that Kiki was, in more ways than one, invaluable. The impassive boy's attendance seemed to be entirely purposeless until, at a nod from the head waiter, he leaned forward and removed the half-finished bottle of Frascati and carried it, with a firm and uncompromising step, to a remote corner of the room. Seconds later, with the same firm and uncompromising step, he returned with a large ice cream, which he set before her, and resumed his position behind her chair. The woman with the dog rolled her fine hieratic eye in Edith's direction, gave a complicated and sophisticated grimace, and returned her attention to her plate. Theatrical, thought Edith; one of those extremely tall dancers who make a go of it in foreign cabarets and then retire. But why here?

She was aware that the food was hot and excellent, and that, much to her surprise, she was enjoying it, reviving minute by minute under its influence. Slightly more alert by now, she looked round the room, but there was little to see; the grey men were still absorbed in their conversation; two young couples, from the town, obviously, having a night out, had been placed near the windows, overlooking the invisible garden. A plump elderly man, who was in fact M. Huber, had decided to keep an eye on things while having his dinner and thus combine his two favourite occupations; although finding almost everything to his taste, M. Huber did not neglect to summon nearly all the waiters to his table, where they were subjected to twinkling admonitions and then speeded on their way. Out of season, reflected Edith, and it is beginning to show. The woman with the dog got up, stumbled, her napkin falling to the floor; then, picking up Kiki, she turned a superb stare on to the boy in the white jacket who had stepped forward, and, taking a deep breath, prepared to make a dignified exit. Mme de Bonneuil, her hands on the table, gave a loud belch. M. Huber closed his eyes briefly, Edith was interested to see, but when he opened them his face creased into an expression of seraphic joy. Following his gaze, she saw the occasion for this. Across the room, in midnight blue lace, small diamonds sparkling in her ears, the glamorous lady who had demanded tea for her daughter stood hesitantly in the doorway; then, having assured herself that her presence had been noted and would indeed be welcomed, she advanced graciously to her table. Her daughter, in a sleeveless black dress, followed after, smiling to left and right, as if to gather up the bouquets.

This I must see, thought Edith, pouring herself another glass of water. She was already aware of powerful and undiagnosed feelings toward these two: curiosity, envy, delight, attraction, and fear, the fear she always felt in the presence of strong personalities. And they were undoubtedly strong, there was no doubt of that, although their presence here was problematic. They seemed destined for better things. This was apparent in the way that waiters appeared from all sides to settle them in their chairs; menus were flourished, laughing remarks exchanged. The woman with the dog, quite eclipsed by this activity, looked back at them with another complicated expression on her face; Edith noted that although she had already encountered the two women on her way out they had quite ignored her. Again, a tiny thrill of fear whispered at the back of her mind. But they were worth watching; they were veritable concentrations of energy, as well as of charm. And not only were they charming to look at, they had glorious appetites to match. Talking busily to each other, knives and forks flashed as they ate their way enthusiastically through four courses; at the same time, plans were being drawn up for the following day. 'What time did you order the car?' Edith could hear, and 'Remind me to take those shoes back, Mummy.' Then, like many greedy women, they sat back fastidiously, as if the food had scarcely come to their notice. Butter wouldn't melt, thought Edith.

Yet she was forced to follow them out, a humble and often stalled attendant in their rosy and perfumed wake (for this, she now realized, was the source of the scent she had smelt in the corridor) and as they took their seats in the salon, she sat near them, as if to gain some bravery, some confidence, from their utterly assured presence. Waiting for coffee to be brought, they surveyed their faces sternly in the mirrors of their respective compacts; adjustments were made, lips gleamed anew, and the ash blonde lady lifted her head to smile at the elderly pianist who had now returned, with further selections from indeterminate sources. 'Ah, Noel,' the ash blonde lady exclaimed indulgently, as the mild and conscientious sound arose. 'What a genius that boy was.'

That *boy*? Edith realized that ages would have to be revised once more, but before she could do this she saw the daughter rise to her feet, smooth her black dress down over her abundant hips, and advance in her direction. Her rather large, flushed, blonde face was lowered quizzically towards Edith, and she said, 'Mummy was wondering if you would like to join us for coffee?'

And of course it was deliverance, deliverance from the evening that lay ahead, and Edith rose joyfully to her feet, followed the daughter, bowed her head slightly to the mother, and said, 'How kind of you. My name is Edith Hope and I only arrived today. I . . .'

'I am Mrs Pusey,' said the lady. 'Iris Pusey.'

'How do you do? Have you been here . . .'

'And this is my daughter, Jennifer.'

They sat down, smiling at each other expectantly. Coffee arrived. Mrs Pusey leaned forward and took her cup. 'I said to Jennifer, do go and ask that lady to join us. I hate to see anyone on their own. Especially in the evening.' She settled back in her chair. Edith smiled again.

'I said, she has such sad eyes.'

3

The next morning, flat calm.

Edith awoke to a mild pinkish dusk. Levering herself up cautiously in the unfamiliar bed, she peered at her watch to try to see the time. She had supposed it to be very early; she remembered waking some time before and hearing a door close quietly some little way down the corridor, but she saw to her surprise that it was nearly eight o'clock, and a finger of light, appearing through the veal-coloured curtains, seemed to contain the promise of a fine day. She rang for breakfast, then got up and pulled the curtains; in her long white nightgown she stepped out onto the little balcony and shivered in the cold air. But the mist was lifting from the lake, and ahead of her, in the far distance, she could see a dark grey shape, which, as she looked, gained in both outline and volume: the mountain. Below her a small boat puttered quietly at the landing stage, and the chef appeared, in his sponge bag trousers and his white jacket, to take the day's delivery of fresh perch.

The impassive boy who had stood behind the chair of the woman with the dog delivered her breakfast tray, sliding it down from shoulder height onto her little table.

'*Merci*,' she said, her voice still unfamiliar to her, for it had not been in use for some time. '*Il fait froid?*'

'*Il a neigé cette nuit sur la montagne*,' he replied austerely.

He seemed to take his tasks so very seriously for one so young. He was, perhaps, eighteen; his hair was punishingly short, and he had the set expression and also the expertise of a much older servant, a gentleman's gentleman, repository of secrets, man of honour in his own right, a worthy servitor to his liege lord.

'*Comment vous appelez-vous?*' she asked gently.

He turned at the door and smiled, revealing a chipped front tooth and the trusting eyes of a boy who has set himself stern tasks but who is glad to be befriended.

'*Alain*,' he replied. '*Je m'appelle Alain.*'

Edith drank her coffee and reflected on the previous evening. Well, something had been accomplished; people were beginning to have names. The here and now, the quotidian, was beginning to acquire substance. The dimension of terror that this realization brought with it – as if knowing the place too well might give her presence there some reality, some validity – was quickly palliated by the extraordinary accumulation of facts, and of such very diverting facts, that had emerged from her meeting with Iris and Jennifer Pusey. Or, rather, with Iris Pusey, for Jennifer was so much a reflection of her mother that although she occupied quite a large space and had a curiously insistent physical presence, she did not have too much to say for herself, and indeed Edith had once or twice had the impression that behind her large smiling face Jennifer was somewhere else.

But in any event Iris held the stage; Iris, it was clear, was the star. Like many a star, she could only function from a position of dominance; she held information at bay, so that Edith was not required to give an account of herself. Edith, having been briefly the recipient of Mrs Pusey's compassion, was now to become Mrs Pusey's confidante. And what a lot there was to tell, Edith reflected. What busy lives some people led. Iris Pusey was putting in her brief annual appearance at the Hotel du Lac for one purpose only; she had come to shop. And she was enabled to do this by virtue of the fact that her late husband had prudently deposited certain sums of money in an account in her name in a Swiss bank.

Edith had learned all this by the end of the first half-hour spent in Mrs Pusey's company. Half an hour was all that was needed for the rules of the game to be set down, the wordless contract agreed upon by both parties. In return for her deliverance from that dread fate so sympathetically observed by Mrs Pusey, Edith was to make herself available when not otherwise engaged – and that engagement would have to be submitted to fairly searching scrutiny – and to provide an audience for Mrs Pusey's opinions, reminiscences, character readings, or general views on life's little problems. Edith acquiesced to this readily enough, not because of her plight, which she saw as irremediable but not entirely serious, but because Mrs Pusey presented her with the opportunity to examine, and to enjoy, contact with an alien species. For in this charming woman, so entirely estimable in her happy desire to capture hearts, so completely preoccupied with the femininity which had always provided her with life's chief delights, Edith perceived avidity, grossness, ardour. It was her perception of this will to repletion and to triumph that had occasioned her mild feeling of faintness when she watched Mrs Pusey and Jennifer eating their dinner. She had also perceived a difference of appetite, one that seemed to carry an implicit threat to her own. Yet she dismissed this as ridiculous (dismissed it also as potentially too painful to contemplate) as she sat drinking coffee in the agreeable company of Jennifer and Mrs Pusey and basking in the high summer of their self-esteem, which in its turn shed a kindly light on all those within its orbit. And to Edith, at this strange juncture in her life, there was something soothing in the very existence of Mrs Pusey, a woman so gentle, so greedy, so tranquil, so utterly fulfilled in her desires that she encouraged daring thoughts of possession, of accumulation, in others. She was, Edith thought, an embodiment of the kind of propaganda no contemporary woman could stoop to countenance, for Mrs Pusey was not only an enchantress in her own right, she was also appreciative of such propensities in others. (She was also, by the same token, dismissive). She had unexpected areas of imagination, of generosity. For example, she saw her daughter not as a rival, as a lesser woman might have done, but as a successor, to be groomed for the stardom which would eventually be hers by right. There was indeed a physical closeness between mother and daughter that surpassed anything Edith had ever known, and there was also love on both sides, although Edith registered that love as being mildly unrealistic. For in spite of Jennifer's physical stolidity, a stolidity which verged on opulence, it was clear that her mother still thought of her as a small girl. And Jennifer, probably now as a matter of habit as well as of fondness, continued to behave like one.

The result of all this was to re-open in Edith's mind the question of what behaviour most becomes a woman, the question around which she had written most of her novels, the question she had attempted to argue with Harold Webb, the question she had failed to answer and which she now saw to be of the most vital importance. The excitement she thus experienced at being provided with an opportunity to study the question at first hand was if anything heightened by the fact that everything that Mrs Pusey had said so far was of the utmost triviality. Clearly there were depths here that deserved her prolonged attention.

Mrs Pusey had conveniently opened the debate by referring to her husband, now unfortunately dead, but still an inspiration to her and ever in her thoughts.

'A wonderful, wonderful man,' she had said, after releasing this information, the thumb and forefinger of her right hand pressed briefly above the bridge of her nose.

'Don't, Mummy,' begged Jennifer, her hand stroking her mother's forearm.

Mrs Pusey gave a shaky little laugh. 'She does hate me to get upset,' she said to Edith. 'It's all right, darling, I'm not going to be silly.' And she pulled out a fine white lawn handkerchief and dabbed at the corners of her mouth.

'Oh, but you can't think how I miss him,' she confided to Edith. 'He gave me everything I could possibly want. My early married life was like a dream. He used to say, "Iris, if it'll make you happy, buy it. I'll give you a blank cheque. And don't spend it all on the house. Spend it on yourself." But of course my lovely home came first. How I adored that house.' Here the thumb and forefinger were once again applied to the bridge of the nose.

'Where do you live?' asked Edith, aware that this was an unimpressively bald question.

'Oh, but my dear, I'm talking about our first home, in Haslemere. Oh, I wish I had the photos here. Architect designed, it was. It was my dream home. And I mustn't talk about it too much, because Jennifer will get upset, won't you, darling? Oh, yes, it broke her heart to leave Green Tiles.'

I can just see it, thought Edith. Parquet floors. Fitted cupboards. Picture windows. Every conceivable appliance in the kitchen. Gardener twice a week. Gardener's wife, devoted, in a white overall, every day. Downstairs cloakroom for the gentlemen to use after playing a round of golf. Patio, she added.

'But when my husband went to Head Office and I saw how much travelling he was going to have to do, I put my foot down. Why should he wear himself out, I said to myself, just to please his silly little wife who loves a quiet life in the country? And anyway, I knew he would want me to entertain for him. I knew that before he did. So we moved to St John's Wood. Montrose Court. And of course it's a beautiful flat, and I have an excellent housekeeper. And it's big enough for Jennifer to have her own suite. She can invite all her friends; I leave her entirely alone. And the shops are very good.'

She dabbed the corners of her mouth again. 'Of course, I have everything delivered,' she added.

Having assured Edith of her comfortable circumstances at home, she went on to describe to her the tenor of their life abroad. It was clear that as travelling companions, Mrs Pusey and Jennifer were entirely compatible. Abroad was seen mainly as a repository for luxury goods. They were extensively familiar with the kind of resort which had recently but definitively gone out of fashion; hence their presence here, although that was also explained by the bank account and the fact that Mr and Mrs Pusey had known M. Huber when they motored over from Montreux 'in the old days'. But it became clear that Mr Pusey had frequently been left at home to do whatever he did while Jennifer and her mother took off for restorative trips to Cadenabbia or Lucerne or Amalfi or Deauville or Menton or Bordighera or Estoril. Once, only once, to Palma, but that was apparently a mistake. 'I never could stand the heat. After that, my husband said he wouldn't risk the Mediterranean again, not in the high season. Of course, that was before all these package tours. Pretty place. But the heat was terrible. I spent all my time in the cathedral, trying to cool down. Never again.'

No, Mrs Pusey went on, she preferred the cooler weather. And they hated crowds. And M. Huber made them so welcome. Of course, they always had the same suite. The one on the third floor, overlooking the lake.

'Then I think we must be on the same corridor,' ventured Edith. 'My room is 307.'

'Why, yes,' said Mrs Pusey. 'That little room at the end. Of course, there are very few single rooms in a place like this.' She looked speculatively at Edith. 'If we go up together, you can look in and see where we are,' she said. Then, urging herself effortfully to the edge of her chair, she attempted to rise, and after two false starts heaved herself upright, shaking off Jennifer's arm and steadying herself on her fine ankles. This woman is getting on for seventy, thought Edith.

But it did not seem so, as she followed the shapely midnight blue back and the wake of rosy scent into the lift and out again and along the corridor. While Jennifer was allowed forward to open the door, Mrs Pusey made herself ready to do the honours. They did indeed have a suite: their two bedrooms could be entered separately from the corridor, but, Mrs Pusey implied, they were invariably to be found in the small salon that connected them and which was agreeably filled with the amenities which confident people accord themselves in strange places: a colour television, a basket of fruit, flowers, several splits of champagne. And leading the way into her bedroom, Mrs Pusey gestured with a smile to a négligé in oyster-coloured satin, thickly encrusted with lace, which was laid out over the

29

back of a chair. 'My weakness,' she confided. 'I do love nice things. And there's such a good shop in Montreux. That's why we come back here every year.'

She eyed Edith again and smiled. 'You should buy yourself something pretty while you're here, dear. A woman owes it to herself to have pretty things. And if she feels good she looks good. That's what I tell Jennifer. I always see to it that she's fitted out like a queen. Don't I, darling?'

And she held out her arms to Jennifer who walked into them and snuggled her face against her mother's. 'Ah,' laughed Mrs Pusey. 'She loves her silly mother, don't you, darling?' And they embraced lovingly and walked to the door, still entwined, to see Edith out. 'Don't be alone, dear,' said Mrs Pusey. 'You know where to find us.' And the door had closed.

Edith found herself thinking about this conversation at various moments in the night when the Spartan firmness of her mattress made her normally light sleep more intermittent than usual. She thought too of the Aladdin's cave she had perceived in the Puseys' suite, with its careless deployment of pleasurable attributes. But most of all she thought of the charming tableau of mother and daughter entwined, their arms locked about each other, their rosy faces turned to Edith. Seeing her, they had taken the full measure of her solitariness, and the implication of this condition showed in their expressions which had become quite innocent with surprise and pity. She had felt almost apologetic as, with a stiff little bow (and that was an association and a reminiscence in itself), she had bid them goodnight and made her way thoughtfully to her room. And had resolved to learn and to do better, so that this particular complex of feelings might not be activated again.

The next morning, dressed in her tweed skirt and her long cardigan, Edith reflected that she had perhaps been a little lax in presenting an appearance to the world. And that if the world had not shown much interest in her appearance ('And what are you working on now?' people asked her at parties) then it was perhaps her fault. She had failed to scale the heights of consumerism that were apparently as open to her as they were to anyone else; this could now be remedied. If a woman feels good she looks good, she said to herself, as she stepped out into the corridor. And as she crossed the foyer and went out through the revolving door, steadying herself with a deep breath before going out into the world, she reminded herself once again of this dictum. Of course, I have everything delivered, she added.

But it was clear after about ten minutes that abroad for her, even a small resort out of season, was not the same as it was for Iris Pusey or even for Jennifer. Where they saw luxury goods, she saw only houses of detention. 'Pension Lartigue (Dir. Mme Vve. Lartigue)' was followed by 'Clinique Les Mimosas (Dr Privat)'. A small railed garden contained two men playing chess on a collapsible table, watched by six totally silent onlookers. Disappointed, but still calm, she walked on until she came to a large café, its glass windows half covered with steam. She went in and sat down, taking a notebook out of her bag to give herself a countenance. But the sight before her was more reassuring. A low buzz of conversation emanated from a number of sturdy-looking women; flushed waitresses carried plates of cakes from a counter to the tables; coffee was ordered and reordered. Somewhere in the distance Edith could hear a familiar little whine; looking up, she saw the tall woman break off a piece of macaroon and poke it into Kiki's mouth. Catching sight of Edith, the tall woman raised her small silver fork in brief and silent greeting. Edith nodded and smiled. What on earth was this woman doing here? Mrs Pusey would no doubt know. And what am I doing here myself, she thought, but quelled that thought, paid her bill, and left.

The rest of her walk yielded no further evidence of the sybaritic life. A small corner shop, evidently a grocery of some sort, displayed on its pavement three perfectly unadorned baskets of string beans. Outside the station she bought a three days old copy of *The Times*. And returning to the hotel she was just in time to see Mrs Pusey and Jennifer being ceremoniously installed in the back of an old-fashioned limousine. Off to Montreux, no doubt, to get Jennifer fitted out like a queen. Edith turned slowly back into the hotel, went up in the lift, met a fresh effusion of scent in the corridor, and sat down thoughtfully at the little table in her room.

'My dearest David,' she wrote,

'Well, it is all go here, a veritable whirl of activity. And an unworldly creature like myself might well have shrunk back in alarm from the sophistication of the smart set, had I not been kindly taken in hand by a respectable duenna, Mrs Iris Pusey of Montrose Court, late of Haslemere. It is thought that I might prove an acceptable companion for her daughter Jennifer, although Jennifer is clearly destined for higher things. However, Jennifer is in no hurry to leave her mother, or so her mother assures me, and in the meantime we are all peaceably pretending that the right man will come along in due course. At the moment, there are no men at all. Apart from Mrs Pusey's husband (who seems to have no other title or appellation, none being needed, it is implied) we are on our own.

'She is quite the most interesting person here, although there is a beautiful woman with a dog who looks promising. Her husband is something important in Brussels, I understand. However, we have not yet spoken. Mrs Pusey, on the other hand, is very communicative, which is rather a blessing because otherwise I . . .' (this sentence she crossed out).

'I adore Mrs Pusey. She is a totally serene, supremely confident woman who has, she laughingly suggests, simply made the best of what the good Lord gave her. She clearly has an enormous amount of money and I am rather interested to find out where this came from. When my husband was moved to Head Office, occasioning that tragic departure from Haslemere, where exactly did he go? What was his Head Office Head Office of? There is a nuance in Mrs Pusey's behaviour, and even something, dare I say it, about the cut of Jennifer's jib, that leads me to suspect that my husband might have been the kind of man who calls a shop a retail outlet. But he was clearly a man of decision. Apart from lodging some of his loot in a Swiss bank, it was he who realized that he could not risk the Mediterranean in the high season. Could not risk it for her, I mean. Did he slip off from time to time for a solitary spree at the tables? Was he a closet member of the Marbella Club? I rather hope so, but there is no evidence to support this.

'Incidentally, although I have been thinking of Mrs Pusey as a lady, I have adjusted this downwards: Mrs Pusey is definitely a woman. "All woman", my husband used to call her. (But he was one of the old school.) And the woman with the dog has to be adjusted upwards to lady, or rather Lady. She, or rather her husband, equally absent, is a member of the ruling class, although Mrs Pusey doesn't think much of his title. Mrs Pusey clearly dislikes Lady X (I do not yet know her name). It will be interesting to find out why.

'But otherwise, we all have names now: Mrs Pusey and Jennifer, of course, and the boy who brings the breakfast is Alain, and the pretty little blonde waitress at teatime is Maryvonne . . .'

Edith laid down her pen. It was all very well to write up Mrs Pusey and Jennifer, but she was still left with that memory of the two women lovingly entwined as they saw her to the door to say goodnight. For there was love there, love between mother and daughter, and physical contact, and collusion about being pretty, none of which she herself had ever known. Her strange mother, Rosa, that harsh disappointed woman, that former beauty who raged so unsuccessfully against her fate, deliberately, wilfully letting herself go, slatternly and scornful, mocking her pale silent daughter who slipped so modestly in and out of her aromatic bedroom, bringing the cups of coffee which her mother deliberately spilled. And shouting, 'Too weak! Too weak! All of you, too weak!' Sighing for Vienna, which had known her young and brilliant, and not fat and slovenly, as she was now. And weeping for her dead sister, Anna.

Thinking of Mrs Pusey's sparkling charm, Edith encountered painful memories. They had aged badly, the fascinating Schaffner sisters, her mother, Rosa, her aunt Anna. They had enslaved many of the students who had lodged in their mother's grim apartment while preparing their theses on Klimt or Schnitzler or the Jugendstil, or on all three. But although the sisters had married promptly, and young, they were soon bitterly disappointed. Those students, so attractive away from home, turned all too soon into mild university men. The campuses of Reading, of Nottingham, of Ohio State, of Kingston, had little to offer two such accomplished Viennese flirts, with their strategies, their tactics, their moods, and their endless desire for victory. When the sisters found each other again, many years later, together with their cousin Resi, it was to outbid each other with stories of horrific boredom, of husbands become too puny to interest them, of pointless days which it seemed beneath them to try to fill. Annoyance and frustration blazed from their every pore; in their mother's dark drawing room the air was filled with dissension, with ugliness. They were now heavy women, punishingly corseted, with badly pencilled eyebrows, and large, hard bosoms. They whipped themselves into a blaze of retrospective fury, voices raised, coffee spilling from their cups. '*Schrecklich! Schrecklich!*' they shouted. '*Ach, du Schreck!*'

Seven-year-old Edith, hiding behind Grossmama Edith's chair, heard with relief her father's key in the door and ran to him, crying. The brutal sound of the words, which she did not understand, hurt her. Her father, guessing, smiled palely, and suggested that they go for a walk. He took her to the Kunsthistorisches Museum and tried to explain the pictures to her, but she pressed her wet red face against his hand and would not listen. And when he stopped longingly before a picture of men lying splayed in a cornfield under a hot sun she burst into further tears, and he bent down and smoothed her hair back from her forehead. Now, Edith, he had said, wiping her eyes with his handkerchief, this is when character tells.

And he had died quite young, in his early fifties, her poor little professor, and scornful Rosa had collapsed without him. Not a day passed as, dirtier and more irascible, she heaped insults upon his memory. But when she in her turn died, not long after, Edith had found among her papers a faded scrap of a letter in her father's careful student German, an invitation of some kind, its purpose now lost, and only its opening sentence hinting at earlier, happier times. In a gentle sloping hand were written the words, 'Gracious lady, would you do me the honour . . .' before the torn paper obliterated the rest of the message.

Edith rubbed her eyes, and picked up her pen again.

'My dear darling, you cannot know how much I think of you and long for you and wait until I can see you again.'

This she blotted carefully and laid aside. Then, taking up the folder containing *Beneath the Visiting Moon*, she pulled out her papers, re-read her last paragraph, and bent her head obediently to her daily task of fantasy and obfuscation.

4

'I think you have an admirer,' said Mrs Pusey with a light laugh.

Edith made no reply, nor, it seemed, was she required to do so, for Mrs Pusey, in an almond green linen coat and skirt, and wearing her daytime pearls, had turned away from her to summon Maryvonne: more hot water was needed.

Edith, emerging dazed and haggard from her room after several hours with *Beneath the Visiting Moon*, had found the salon deserted with the exception of Mme de Bonneuil, who was reading very small portions of the *Gazette de Lausanne* through a magnifying glass. The dense, warm silence of the place indicated that she was too late for lunch and too early for tea. She crossed the foyer, still mildly anaesthetized by her labours, and stepped again through the revolving door into an afternoon of such mature beauty that she wondered how she could possibly have missed it. An autumn sun, soft as honey, gilded the lake; tiny waves whispered onto the shore; a white steamer passed noiselessly off in the direction of Ouchy; and at her feet, on the sandy path, she saw the green hedgehog shape of a chestnut, split open to reveal the brown gleam of its fruit.

The café with the clouded windows, now transparent and bathed in afternoon light, was almost empty. Seated at a silent table, Edith closed her eyes momentarily in a shaft of sunlight and tasted pure pleasure. Time dissolved; sensations expanded. She drank coffee, still too highly charged with vicarious emotion to eat, and then sat back in her chair, her eyes closed once more, savouring the reward of rest after her obscure and unnoticeable exertions. When she opened her eyes it was to see the extraordinary sight of the woman with the dog, remote, on the shore of the lake, bending and uncoiling her long narrow body, her slender arm flung out from time to time, her hair shining and tousled, her strange cry, 'Kiki! Kiki!', just audible through the window as the little dog, his neurotic temperament forgotten, chased after sticks. The lonely energy of the woman, the wild strangeness and concentration of her gesture, changed Edith's mood back into one of caution, and she retraced her steps back to the hotel, returned to the melancholy of exile.

Tea was being served, and to Edith's surprise it was being served to a number of people whom she had not seen before. More young waiters than she had previously noticed were busy at tables filled by groups of men in high good humour, animated by cordial discussion; one or two looked up as she passed, then returned to the more urgent matter of business that had brought them here, from the conference in Geneva, for a last informal meeting before they all went their separate ways. For the first time, Edith was aware of the hotel as a well populated organism, its attendants merely resting until an appropriate occasion should summon them to present them-selves, serious and anxious to give service, at an appointed time. That time, it seemed, had now arrived. M. Huber, at the desk, getting in his son-in-law's way, smiled, nodded, and suggested difficult alterations to the menu for dinner.

To this scene of animation, her nose wrinkling slightly at the unusual smell of cigarette smoke, came Mrs Pusey, late as usual, and perhaps a little tired after a day which had not yielded the required amount of shopping. They had been after a particular kind of blouse, with drawn-thread work, she explained to Edith, who was drawn to Mrs Pusey's table from her own as if by some magnetic force, but there had been a disappointment. The little woman who used to make the blouses had just disappeared, without giving them any sort of notice, although she was well aware that Mrs Pusey and Jennifer came over every year and always gave her a substan-tial order. *And* sent her a Christmas card. 'But there you are,' said Mrs Pusey. 'The old days of service have disappeared, even in Switzerland. It's not my world any longer.' She gave a little smile. 'No, everything has changed, and not for the better, either. But one thing I will *not* do is lower my standards. I have always striven for the best. It's an instinct, I suppose. As my husband used to say, Only the best is good enough.'

'Mummy,' cried Jennifer hotly. 'You *are* the best.' She grasped her mother's hand, and both sets of eyes took on the brave glisten of the recently bereaved, although even if the bereavement was occasioned by the disloyal specialist in drawn-thread work, Edith reflected, there was little she could offer in the way of consolation. While the, to her, extraordinary communion between mother and daughter was demonstrated once again, she studied Jennifer, who always seemed to her as inexpressive as a blank window, although all her gestures were vigorous and all her interventions emphatic. Jennifer was a splendid specimen, she acknowledged, an effortless testimonial to her mother's care. Her large fair face, perhaps a little too sparsely populated by a cluster of rather small features, shone with the ruddy health of an unsuspecting child. Everything about her gleamed. Her light blue eyes, her regular, slightly incurving teeth, her faultless skin, all gave off various types of sheen; her blonde hair looked almost dusty in comparison. Her rather plump artless body was, Edith saw, set forth by clothes which were far from artless and possibly too narrow; Jennifer managed to give the impression that she was growing out of them. Everything about her was as expensive as her mother's money could make it, but in a different style from Mrs Pusey's careful elegance. In her navy linen trousers and her, perhaps too tight, white jersey, Jennifer was determinedly *gamine*. Edith wondered how old she was. She looked very young, as did Mrs Pusey, but in a way she could not define they were both out of date. They referred almost constantly to times gone by, times illuminated by glamour, happiness, success, confidence, and security, times of necessity remote and mysterious to their interlocutor. Edith reflected how enormously one-sided conversations with the Puseys were always likely to be. They imposed their past as deliberately as they did their present, and to both of these one was expected, in some curious way, to pay homage. They required no information at all; once they had assured themselves that Edith was alone, they had requisitioned her, and this was not only a kindness but a convenience, proof, to Edith's mind, of sophisticated thinking. And as most of Mrs Pusey's sentences began with the words 'Of course', they had a range of tranquil confidence which somehow occluded any attempt to introduce an opinion of her own. She found all this amusing and very restful; the last thing she wanted to do was to talk about herself. No, not that. But she confessed to herself that she was somewhat disturbed by Jennifer's cheerful but steady refusal of any kind of mutuality. After all, she thought, we are almost of an age, although she is a few years younger. She might be, what? Thirty-two? Thirty-three? Possibly thirty-four? And yet she belongs to her mother, as if her mother had been cast upon an uncaring and philistine world and it was Jennifer's duty to protect her from it. What Jennifer felt about this few people were likely to find out, Edith thought, as she observed, while Mrs Pusey was talking, Jennifer's uninflected smile.

At this point in her musings she was disturbed by a pleasant male voice saying, 'Don't lose this', and offering her the notebook which must have slipped from her lap unnoticed while she was contemplating Jennifer. Startled, she looked up to see a tall man in a light grey suit smiling down at her. She murmured her thanks, expecting him to go away; she could hardly ask him to sit down and join them. But, 'Are you a writer?' he enquired, in a voice very slightly tinged with amusement. As if he *knew*, thought Edith, in some confusion, although the idea that anyone could be a writer in a place like this was not likely to be taken seriously. Or so she hoped. She gave a distracted smile, intending to deflect further questions, and, still looking amused, he moved away and followed his friends or colleagues out, away from the tea tables, into the fresh air.

'It seems you have an admirer,' said Mrs Pusey. And when more hot water arrived she added, 'He's had his eye on you since you came in. I saw it at once.' She spoke roguishly, but her eyelids drooped, as if this merely added to the day's disappointments. Jennifer, Edith saw, was still glassily smiling.

It was time to go up and change and yet they lingered on. Edith felt constrained by a kind of loyalty to wait upon Mrs Pusey, although it was not quite clear to her why loyalty was involved. Their silence was ruminative; no confidences were to be offered or exchanged. Just what I wanted, Edith reminded herself, but what she suddenly longed to do was to speak to David; the intrusion of a man into her consciousness, however parodic, had the painful effect of awakening her longing. She glanced at her watch, calculating the time anxiously; if she rushed upstairs now, she might just catch him before he left. At the Rooms, she thought, with a pang of love and terror.

'I must be getting back to the Rooms,' were the first words she had consciously heard him say, and she was struck by their mystery. She turned the amazing sentence over in her mind, conjuring up vistas of courtyards with fountains trickling and silent servants in gauze trousers bringing sherbet. Or possibly large divans in whitewashed houses shuttered against the heat of the afternoon, a dreaming, glowing idleness, inspired by Delacroix. Or of grave merchants, with clicking amber beads, in coffee houses below pavement level. Opium dens. Turkish baths. A tiled hammam, its walls bright with coins of light reflected from the water. Peace.

'What do you do?' she enquired, her eyes wide with this vision, gazing off into the middle distance.

'I am an auctioneer,' he replied. And then there had been a brief silence.

They had met at one of her friend Penelope Milne's irritating little parties. 'Drinks before lunch next Sunday,' came the inexorable voice over the telephone. 'Now don't let me down. You can work in the afternoon if you want to. I'm not stopping you.'

But you are, thought Edith. Since you are too mean to

provide any food, and since I don't care to eat at half-past two or whenever I get back with a splitting headache, my day is effectively ruined. And Penelope had such a curious attitude to providing food; she regarded it as some sort of unseemly submission. Her company could only be purchased via the old and hoary routes of flowers, theatre tickets, and intimate dinners at the best restaurants, of which she was a connoisseur. To Penelope, men were conquests, attributes, but they were also enemies; they belonged to the species that must never be granted more than the amount of time and attention she considered they deserved. Her tone with such men was flirtatious, mocking, never serious; she spread about her a propaganda of rapid affairs, rapidly consummated, with a laughing lack of commitment on both sides. She seemed to take a pride in the steady succession of names. She was, Edith saw, accomplished in venery. And as an accompaniment, she was given to sighing elaborately over Edith's uneventful life and was clearly of the opinion that Edith only wrote about those pleasures that reality had denied her. She was generous with offers to introduce Edith to various grass-widowers of her acquaintance – 'my cast-offs', as she laughingly referred to them – and was piqued when Edith pleaded that she was really no company when she was working on a book. She would have taken pleasure, Edith knew, in setting up a meeting, with herself present; she would have master-minded Edith, with many a jocund reference to her own successes with the amiable candidate; she would even have ushered them off the premises to a restaurant of her own choosing, would have whispered something in the cast-off's ear, and then said firmly to Edith, 'I'll ring you in the morning.' Yet she considered men to be a contemptible sex, and her eyes would sparkle when she recounted tales of conquest at the various committee meetings which were the very stuff of her social life. 'That dreadful little man,' she would say dismissively, of someone who did not know the rules of her game.

She was a handsome woman of forty-five and would remain

so for many years. She and Edith had in common the dispositions of their houses, for they were at opposite ends of the tiny terrace, their domestic arrangements, which consisted of the window-cleaner (not to be missed; they had each other's keys), and Mrs Dempster, their dramatic and unpredictable cleaning lady. There was an understanding between them that if either were ill the other would shop and cook. This last contingency had not yet arisen but was of a comfort to them both. Edith, tired, yawning, aching from her silent day, would push away her typewriter, wander out of her house and into Penelope's, and be quite happy to advise her on what to wear on her next sortie. Penelope, though never referring to the matter of Edith's work, would push her forward, as if she were a child, at her all too frequent parties, and say, 'And of course you know Edith Hope. She writes.' Such was their friendship.

On this particular Sunday Penelope had drummed up a good attendance and there were many people there whom Edith did not know. She resigned herself to standing around for the requisite amount of time (Penelope did not like one to sit down) when the resonant sentence floated into her consciousness. Tracing it to its source, she saw a tall, lean, foxy man helping himself to a handful of peanuts; she saw, from his back, that he was restless, impatient, and burning to get away. Any excuse would do. Hence his improbable, his implausible remark, which was followed, rather too fluently, in the teeth of Penelope's protests, by an account of a late catalogue entry which demanded his urgent attention.

Edith, still filled with her vision of the hammam, the Arab café, the Mediterranean siesta, murmured somewhat distractedly, as he made his determined way to the door, 'Could you describe these Rooms to me?'

He contemplated her from a considerable height, down a long nose. 'A five-storey warehouse in Chiltern Street,' he said.

Then she looked up at him and they exchanged a level glance from which all expression was studiously absent. She lowered her eyes, and he left. Nothing more was said.

Later, as she was helping Penelope to wash the glasses, she had asked, 'That tall man, what does he do?'

'David Simmonds? He's head of the family business, now. Simmonds, the auction house. They handle a lot of the bigger country house sales. Rather a pet, isn't he? He's always been a bit keen on me, but he's so hard to get hold of these days. He asked about you, by the way.'

'How do you know him?' said Edith.

'I was at school with his wife,' said Penelope. 'Priscilla. You know. You've met her here a dozen times. *You* know, Edith. Tall, blonde, very good-looking. She couldn't come today.'

Edith did remember her: tall, blonde, very good-looking. A woman with a rather insolent air of authority, of carelessness. A loud, confident voice. She had once encountered her in the china department at Peter Jones and had noticed the way she bounced along, trailing an assistant, like a favoured senior girl in the school common room.

Penelope removed her plastic apron imprinted with an advertisement for Guinness and pegged up her rubber gloves. 'Now, Edith, I'm afraid I'm going to have to turn you out. Richard said he'd come back and take me out to lunch round the corner.'

Edith, at her window, watched Richard turn up, sprinting down the road with commendable alacrity. Spry, she thought. Jaunty. Good check suit straining slightly over wide back. Veined hand waving. She pictured David and smiled involuntarily. She sat down to wait for him.

When he came, as she knew he would, two or three hours later, they said nothing but looked at each other long and hard. In bed, they fell instantly into a warm mutual sleep, arms around each other, and when they woke, almost simultaneously, they had laughed with pleasure. After that, it seemed as if she knew everything about him; the only revelation was his delightful and constant appetite. She took to keeping the house full of food.

They were sensible people. No one was to be hurt. She

prided herself on giving nothing away, so that he never knew of her empty Sundays, the long eventless evenings, the holidays cancelled at the last minute. Cursing inwardly, as he loaded the car for the long journey back from Suffolk, after another crowded and inharmonious weekend, he thought of her little house, its quality of silence, the green dimness of her drawing room. She, too early in bed, thought of him with his family, their habits, their quarrels, their treats. Of his children.

And thinking of this, yet again, in the Hotel du Lac, she felt the ache in her throat that preceded tears (but she was so good at concealing them), and murmuring an excuse to Mrs Pusey, she took the unprecedented step of leaving the salon before her. She would make no telephone call. She was, after all, if not still in disgrace, working out her probation.

The tears that had fallen from her fine light eyes seemed to have sharpened her vision. When, some two hours later, she sat down to dinner, she was aware that the lights were brighter, the room more alive with personalities, the tables full. It was agreeable to see men, after days in this gyneceum, bringing the place to life, to see waiters speeding to their command. The man in grey, who had picked up her notebook, half rose as she took her seat, nodded, and then applied his attention to the removal of the backbone from his sole. The woman with the dog looked amazing in a floating flowered chiffon dress, its narrow straps tied into two tiny bows on the beautiful bones of her ivory shoulders. Edith was grateful for the warmth, the food, the service; she felt very tired, and thought that she would sleep soundly that night.

Mrs Pusey, in black chiffon, stood hesitant in the doorway, as if overcome by the excitement, hardly daring to make her way unaccompanied to her table, Jennifer standing mildly behind her. It was only when M. Huber came forward, gallantly holding out his hand, that Mrs Pusey broke into a smile, and allowed herself to be led forward. The woman with the dog let out a snort which Mrs Pusey chose not to hear.

Edith, once again anonymous, and accepting her anonymity,

made an appropriately inconspicuous exit. And, sitting in the deserted salon, the first to arrive from the dining room, she felt her precarious dignity hard-pressed and about to succumb in the light of her earlier sadness. The pianist, sitting down to play, gave her a brief nod. She nodded back, and thought how limited her means of expression had become: nodding to the pianist or to Mme de Bonneuil, listening to Mrs Pusey, using a disguised voice in the novel she was writing and, with all of this, waiting for a voice that remained silent, hearing very little that meant anything to her at all. The dread implications of this condition made her blink her eyes and vow to be brave, to do better, not to give way. But it was not easy.

Drinking her coffee in the salon, Edith felt purged by her grief, obedient and childlike, as she had on so many occasions, reaching back into the mists of childhood, to that visit, perhaps, to the Kunsthistorisches Museum with her father. And, childishly anxious to please, she went forward, when the signal came, to join the Puseys at their table. The man in grey had positioned himself nearby, and although purporting to read a newspaper, was almost visibly listening to their conversation. Perhaps he is a detective, thought Edith, without much interest.

'You know, dear,' said Mrs Pusey, after she had repaired her face and received compliments on her appearance, 'You remind me of someone. Your face is very familiar. Now who can it be?'

'Virginia Woolf?' offered Edith, as she always did on these occasions.

Mrs Pusey took no notice. 'It'll come to me in a minute,' she said. 'You two girls talk among yourselves.' And she placed the thumb and forefinger of her right hand to the bridge of her nose, assuming an expression of such gravity that Jennifer, always on the look-out, stopped listening to what Edith was saying and turned her attention to her mother. Edith lay back in her chair and listened to the pianist, who was being ignored by everyone else, until she was aware of

Jennifer's face being lowered into her sightline. 'Mummy says she wants to watch television, so we're going upstairs.' She turned back to her mother and watched the always difficult negotiation from seated to standing position. Again, Edith wondered about her age.

At the door Mrs Pusey turned dramatically, and said, 'I've remembered! I've remembered who Edith reminds me of!'

Edith observed a slight spasm contracting the back of the man in grey, still behind his newspaper.

'Princess Anne!' cried Mrs Pusey. 'I knew it would come to me. Princess Anne!'

5

But sleep did not come easily that night. Between disjointed dreams there flashed onto the cinema screen in Edith's head short audio-visual messages which she would later have to decode. The fine ankles, the unexpected evening pumps of the man in grey. His decision, at some forgotten point, to fold that unconvincing newspaper, to get up, stretch himself slightly, and follow a colleague into the bar. The unusual sounds of merriment that were perceptible, even across the width of the salon, from the direction of the bar. The emergence from the bar, an hour later, of the woman with the dog, helpless with laughter and somewhat dishevelled, her arms linked in those of the man in grey and his friend. Kiki's tiny head raised mournfully at this apostasy, his spherical body attempting to bar her path. A mild altercation between M. Huber and his son-in-law at this sight. The nervous withdrawal of the pianist. His placating smiles all round, to which only Mme de Bonneuil responded with a slight nod.

This information remained in many ways obscure. She was not sure whether she had in fact remained downstairs to witness the scenes which came into her mind, or whether, in some over-active recess of her brain, she was making them up. She was aware that her night was agitated, that the only alternative to waking up was to undergo more of these strange sequences, half dream, half memory. Everything seemed vivid, potent with significance. But the significance was hidden. She stretched uneasily, a prisoner of her troubled sleep. Some-where, at some level of consciousness, she heard a door close.

When she awoke, rather later than usual, it was with the ancient and deadly foreknowledge that the day would be a write-off. Her broken night had left her with an aching head and a instinctive shrinking from both food and company. Minute noises seemed magnified: a trolley was wheeled vigor-ously along the corridor, and the high voices of the maids

47

sounded unbearably piercing. As she took a bath, feeling as unwieldy as an invalid, she drilled herself into a regime of prudence. Depression hovered and must be forestalled. Writing was out of the question. Take things very quietly, she counselled herself: do not think. Close doors.

The pulled curtains revealed another brilliant day, the mountain, with its thin seams of snow, as clear as if it were a few metres distant. Traffic seemed to be in abeyance; a different sort of activity was under way. Outside, in the garden, waiters in clean white jackets placed small chairs and tables beneath the glass awning of the terrace and were even now discussing the advisability of drawing down the orange blinds to palliate the heat of the sun, already palpable through the glass. Somewhere in the distance a toneless bell struck. Sunday, she thought with surprise.

Contingency plans, of the sort at which she had become adept, were called for. Perhaps she could simply sit in the sun and read. She was not likely to be disturbed. Contingency plans were no doubt at that very moment being perfected in other rooms: she imagined the conversations. Mrs Pusey and Jennifer would be ordering the car to take them out some-where, perhaps; she imagined a scenic drive, culminating in a gourmet lunch. The men from Geneva would get together for some sort of excursion, perhaps across the lake, to Evian. Mme de Bonneuil would be one of the few to stay, reading and silent, as usual. The tall thin beauty with the dog was never visible in the daytime and it was impossible to imagine her doing anything except eating ice cream and smoking, like a child on an exeat from school. Edith thought it entirely prob-able that she would have the day to herself, a prospect which she almost welcomed. Embroiled in her fictional plot, the main purpose of which was to distance those all too real circum-stances over which she could exert no control, she felt a weariness that seemed to preclude any enthusiasm, any initiative, any relaxation. Fiction, the time-honoured resource of the ill-at-ease, would have to come to her aid, but the choice of a book presented some difficulties, since when she was writing she could only read something she had read before, and in her exhausted state, a febrile agitation, invisible to the naked eye, tended to distance even the very familiar. Words became distorted: 'pear', for instance, would become 'fear'. She dreaded making nonsense of something precious to her, and, regretfully, disqualified Henry James. Nothing too big would do, nothing too small would suffice. In any event, her attention was fragmented. In the end she picked up a volume of short stories, the beautifully named *Ces plaisirs, qu'on nomme, à la légère, physiques*. Colette, that sly old fox, would, she trusted, see her through.

Silence reigned on the terrace although it was not empty. At one end sat Mme de Bonneuil, wearing a beige dress and jacket, slightly stained in the front, and a battered beige hat. Her stick planted between her legs, she kept her eyes fixed on the road, a large brown bag placed in readiness on the table beside her. At the other end, entirely silent, stretched out on a chaise longue, and immobile behind very large dark glasses, lay the woman with the dog.

The beautiful day had within it the seeds of its own fragility: it was the last day of summer. Sun burned out of a cloudless blue sky: asters and dahlias stood immobile in the clear light, a light without glare, without brilliance. Trees had already lost the dark heavy foliage of what had been an exceptional August and early September and were all the more poignant for the dryness of their yellowing leaves which floated noiselessly down from time to time. Stepping out from the salon, M. Huber rubbed his hands with pleasure. There would be many occasional visitors for lunch and tea today. But at the moment all was quiet. Nobody spoke. The only sound was the occasional fall of a chestnut.

The man in grey, dressed today in something paler and even more elegant, with, Edith was delighted to note, a panama hat in his hand, stepped out into the garden and surveyed the scene. Catching sight of the woman with the dog, he went

49

across to her, bent over her supine body, and made some apparently jocular enquiry: a weak raising of a very white arm and a long limp hand were his answer. Nodding to Edith and also to Mme de Bonneuil, the man in grey departed on business of his own, his occasional and secret smile once again in evidence.

As he rounded the corner the woman with the dog shot upright, leaned in Edith's direction, and whispered urgently, 'I say! I say! I'm sorry, I don't know your name. Could you be an angel and come and sit with me? I don't want that man round me again today and I simply can't put him off without making a scene, which I've half a mind to do, I can assure you.'

Obediently, and with only the mildest of lingering regrets, Edith closed her book and moved along the terrace, placing herself on a small chair at the head of the chaise longue. Such a lovely peaceful day, she thought. Oh, well. At least she hasn't got the dog with her.

'Monica,' said the woman, extending her narrow, boneless hand.

'Edith,' said Edith, shaking it cautiously. Better not get in too far, she said to herself.

'I've been wondering about you,' said Monica. 'I've wanted to talk to you but you've always been with Ma Pusey and I can't stand the sight of her.'

'Where is she?' asked Edith, wishing that the other would lower her voice. She half expected Mrs Pusey to materialize, clothed in white samite, mystic, wonderful, to restore her own sense of order and hierarchy, and also to inaugurate the day's legitimate distractions.

'God knows. At least they can't be out buying knickers today. Oh, I *beg* your pardon. Lingerie.' She pronounced the word with an exaggeratedly French accent. 'Although I wouldn't put it past her to wake someone up and get them to open the shop just because she happened to have a couple of thousand spare francs about her.'

'There does seem to be a great deal of money,' murmured Edith, in what she hoped was a neutral tone. Servants must feel like this, she reflected, gossiping below stairs.

'Loaded,' said the other. 'Trade, of course. Darling Daddy left them a packet. Wine,' she added, responding to Edith's curiosity. 'He was a sherry importer. And the funny thing is, the old girl can't stand the taste of it. She only likes champagne. Well, who doesn't?'

Edith, remembering the last occasion on which she had drunk champagne, shuddered.

'Anything wrong?' asked Monica.

I am tired, thought Edith. I must be careful. I am not going to confide in this languid and luxurious woman, who would in any case be bored if I did. Light conversation is all that is called for.

'I'm fine,' she said. 'But where is Kiki?'

Monica's face fell. 'In disgrace. Locked in the bathroom. Well, you can't expect a little dog like that to behave as well as he would with his own things around him. And the Swiss hate dogs. That's what's wrong with them, if you ask me.'

'Have you been here long?' asked Edith.

'Ages,' sighed Monica. 'I'm here for my health.'

'Oh, I'm so sorry. Have you been ill?'

'No,' replied the other. 'Look, let's have some coffee, shall we?' She summoned a shadowy waiter with an imperious hand. 'It's so nice to have someone to talk to,' she said. She seemed to be recovering a long-lost animation by the second, and when the coffee arrived, poured it out largely and carelessly, although she took only one sip from her cup and almost immediately lit an immensely long cigarette with a lighter that sprang into a two-inch flame. Everything about her seemed exaggerated: her height, the length of her extraordinary fingers, her carrying voice, her huge oyster-coloured eyes, today slightly bloodshot, Edith could see, behind her dark glasses. A breakdown, she decided. A bereavement. Tread carefully.

Monica nodded towards the cigarette. 'Forbidden, of course. Strict instructions. To hell with it.' She inhaled deeply, as if about to submerge in several fathoms of water. After a few seconds, two plumes of smoke emerged from perfect nostrils. A patch on a lung, perhaps, thought Edith, revising. And how beautiful she is. I had not thought so before.

The sound of wheels on gravel brought their heads round. Mme de Bonneuil, her pug face creased into a smile, was struggling to her feet. A car door banged, and a man walked jauntily into the garden, followed by a woman in a red dress, the spikes of her high-heeled sandals plunging into the lawn. '*Eh bien, maman*,' cried the man, falsely cheery. Kisses were exchanged.

'Poor old trout,' said Monica, her tone very slightly lower. 'She lives for that son. She'd do anything for him. And he comes to see her once a month, takes her out in the car, brings her back, and forgets her.'

'Why is she here?' asked Edith.

Monica shrugged. 'His idea entirely. He considers her manners too rustic for her to be allowed to live under the same roof as that frightful wife of his who, incidentally, started life as a hairdresser before snaffling her first husband. This one's her second. Mme de Bonneuil had a beautiful house near the French border: it's quite a good family, incidentally. Naturally, the daughter-in-law wanted the house to herself. So the old girl had to go. She can't stand the wife, of course. Despises her. Quite right. She lives here because she doesn't want to see the son unhappy.'

'How do you know all this?' asked Edith, startled and impressed.

'She told me,' said Monica, inhaling from another cigarette.

'I've never heard her say a single word,' mused Edith.

'Well, it's difficult for her.' To Edith's enquiring glance Monica replied, 'She's stone deaf. What a life.'

They watched the man and his wife manoeuvring Mme de Bonneuil into the back of the car. A regrettable pair, thought

Edith. The man was chunkily built, swarthy, with dark glasses. He looked like a croupier, off duty until nightfall. The wife was much younger, black-haired, voluptuous, expensive. She will marry yet again, thought Edith, as the car drove off. Then perhaps Mme de Bonneuil can go home. But it seemed unlikely.

Monica, she reflected later, as they strolled slowly along the lake shore, knows far more than I do; it is right that she resembles a sphinx. The morning had passed quite pleasantly in her company. But she was puzzled by Monica's insistence that they visit the café for more coffee and cakes. 'It's nearly lunchtime,' she protested. A fleetingly oblique look crossed Monica's face. 'Oh, come on,' she begged. 'It's Sunday. And I'm sick of that awful fish.'

Watching Monica plunging a resolute fork into an éclair, Edith reflected, with some humility, that she was not good at human nature. She could make up characters but she could not decipher those in real life. For the conduct of life she required an interpreter. And this woman was very pleasant, very pleasant indeed. Although apt, she could see, to cause dissension. M. Huber had frowned when he saw her veer off in the direction of the café, Edith in her wake.

'The one I can't make out', said Edith shamelessly, as Monica leaned back and sucked smoke hungrily from yet another cigarette, 'is Jennifer.'

Monica's fine oval eyes emptied of all expression. 'Jennifer,' she pronounced. And after a pause. 'Jennifer, I assure you, is entirely straightforward.'

Edith, glancing at her watch, saw that it was nearly one o'clock, and, 'We must go,' she said firmly. Monica's face dropped into its habitual lines of obstinate gloom. No dramatics, please, thought Edith. 'Come,' she said, stretching out her hand as the other sat there immobile, shoulders hunched. 'You are much more beautiful when you smile. And it's such a lovely day. Won't you walk back with me?' Slowly, reluctantly, Monica allowed herself to be led to the door, a

53

small smile not quite brought to birth. A mystery here, thought Edith.

When they got back to the Hotel du Lac they found Mrs Pusey and Jennifer sitting on the terrace with the unknown man in the panama hat. A bottle of champagne lolled in a bucket on the table.

'There she is,' called Mrs Pusey in a musical voice. 'Come and join us, dear. We've been looking for you.' She ignored Monica who pursed her lips, donned her glasses, and flung herself disdainfully on to her chaise longue.

Edith, annoyed on behalf of her new friend, hesitated, but was saved by the appearance of waiters, napkins over their arms, in the doorways. Mrs Pusey (who was indeed in white) saw them and became intent on the business of levering herself out of her chair. The man in the panama hat offered his arm and, with Jennifer holding her mother's jacket, they processed into the dining room.

'Come on, Monica,' urged Edith. But Monica pulled down the corners of her mouth, raised a limp hand again, and then to all intents and purposes fell asleep.

The afternoon continued golden and mellow. The beauty of this perfect day brought them all back to the terrace where Edith, to whom Monica presented a stony profile and tightly shut eyes, joined the Puseys and the man with the panama hat, who was introduced as Mr Neville. An hour passed quietly, for Mr Neville had procured English Sunday newspapers from some unknown source and had kindly passed them round. But Mrs Pusey, after flicking distractedly through the pages of the colour supplements, gave a sigh and said, 'Such an ugly world. Greed and sensationalism. Cheap sex. And no taste. Not a sign. Run upstairs and get my book, would you, darling?'

'Yes,' she went on, as Edith and Mr Neville made polite but sustained efforts to ignore this interruption. 'I'm afraid I'm a romantic.' With this pronouncement she smiled at them, as, reluctantly, they surrendered the *Observer*, the *Sunday Times*, the

Sunday Telegraph. 'You see, I was brought up to believe in the right values.' Here we go, thought Edith, swallowing a tiny yawn. 'Love means marriage to me,' pursued Mrs Pusey. 'Romance and courtship go together. A woman should be able to make a man worship her.' Mr Neville inclined his head, giving polite consideration to this view. 'Well, perhaps I've been fortunate,' Mrs Pusey added with a little laugh, looking down to rearrange the bow of her silk blouse. 'My husband worshipped me. Thank you, darling,' she said, as Jennifer handed her a paperback with a straining Art Nouveau profile on the cover. 'This is the sort of story I enjoy,' she went on. She was able to talk even when she was reading, Edith noted.

'*The Sun at Midnight*,' pronounced Mr Neville gravely. 'By Vanessa Wilde. Not a writer known to me,' he said to Edith, watching her profile as she gazed distantly over the lake.

'Although I don't think this is one of her best,' said Mrs Pusey.

Edith felt an author's pang. I was actually quite pleased with that one, she thought. David was on his summer holiday, she remembered, lying fretfully on a Greek beach with his wife. I imagined him to be having a marvellous time and I wrote for ten hours a day to stop myself thinking of him. I was rather proud of myself. Three years ago, already.

As her colour faded and her eyes took on their haze of reminiscence ('You need glasses, Edith!' Penelope would say), Mr Neville leaned forward.

'After I have ordered tea for these ladies,' he said, 'I wonder if you would care to walk a little? It is too good a day to waste. We may not get another like it.'

Edith paused. 'Yes, you go, dear,' said Mrs Pusey in a remote voice, as if to signify the intensity of her reading. 'I expect we'll see you after dinner.'

A crowded day, thought Edith, grateful for the silence of her companion, as they walked slowly away from the little town, along the water's edge. The castle, dour, grim, a rebarbative

55

silhouette, a corrective to the dazzle of the water, occupied a spit of land which advanced into the lake as if to impede further progress. Soon it would obliterate the sun, and its massive shape would darken and seem to advance towards them. Instinctively they stopped, unwilling to witness this ritual extinction, and turned to the parapet, over which they leaned. The day was very slowly losing its colour, the blue of the sky whitening in that neutral hour which signifies the end of the afternoon. The sadness that comes with the approach of evening stole over Edith. Her companion glanced at her. 'Shall we sit down for a moment?' he suggested, guiding her to a stone bench. Crossing his elegant ankles, he asked her permission to light a small cigar.

'Now, Mrs Woolf,' he said. 'I don't believe we've been properly introduced. Philip Neville,' he added calmly.

Edith shot him a sharp glance, for the first time registering his existence above ankle level and the profile usually presented to her as he gave his attention to Mrs Pusey.

'Or may I call you Vanessa Wilde?' he went on.

For the first time in weeks Edith laughed. The sound, so long unheard, surprised her. Once started, she could not stop. Mr Neville surveyed her with a pleased expression as submerged gusts found their way to the surface. Finally, he joined in, his smile lingering while Edith wiped her eyes.

'Now that, if I may say so, was a considerable improvement on your usual expression.'

Edith looked at him in surprise. 'I wasn't aware that anyone was interested in my expression,' she said. 'I rather thought I was useful as an audience, but only as a lay figure is useful to a painter: both can be put aside when no longer required.'

'And you think of yourself as a lay figure?'

'No. That is how others think of me.'

'And you are required to be seen and not heard?'

'I am required to listen and not speak.'

'Then for someone who is not speaking, you are giving away volumes of information.'

'I was not aware . . .'

'How stately you are. I don't mean that you can be seen to be mopping and mowing. I don't imagine you do much of that.'

'Don't be too sure,' said Edith, suddenly sombre.

'No, no. I don't perceive you as a distracted being. I mean that if I were younger and more trendy I should probably say that I could deconstruct the signifiers of your discourse.'

Edith gave a grudging smile.

'That's better. I should say that you were rather bored.'

The mildness, the approximate kindness of this remark, brought a flush to her cheeks. She took a deep and steadying breath, then, her eyes brilliant, she nodded at him.

'Quite,' he said. 'Quite. Then I suggest we go out one day soon. Do you know the hills to the south of us?'

She shook her head.

'Wine-growing country,' he said. 'And there are some very good restaurants. I'll telephone you, if I may.'

They retraced their steps to the hotel. On the terrace, Mrs Pusey and Jennifer were about to take their leave. Non-committal gestures were exchanged. Of Monica there was no sign. Mme de Bonneuil, her smile now tinged with anxiety, sat while her son and daughter-in-law discussed matters common only to themselves in loud voices which she could not hear. Finally, her son, responding to a cocked head and an 'On s'en va?' from his wife, stood up with alacrity and prepared to leave. His wife offered her cheek to her mother-in-law and tripped off to the car. Mme de Bonneuil attempted to retain her son but the car horn sounded, and 'J'arrive,' he called, kissing his mother noisily on both cheeks. Mme de Bonneuil remained standing on the terrace, gazing in the direction of her vanished son, until the silence in which she spent her days was palpable even to Edith and Mr Neville.

That evening, at dinner, at her solitary table, Edith felt her smile returning from time to time. She drank her coffee with the Puseys and made her excuses early. She was, in effect, pleasantly tired and somewhat more contented than usual.

'Jennifer,' urged Mrs Pusey, 'do ask that nice Mr Neville to join us. All on his own, poor man.'

But Mr Neville could and would look after himself, thought Edith, and made her way, smiling, to the door.

There was a moon, she noticed, opening her thick curtains and stepping out on to her balcony, and the air was like milk. She sat for a little while, turning many thoughts over in her mind. A beautiful night, pleasant, calm. Calmer than most. She felt well, and when she eventually moved inside to the mirror to brush her hair, she thought, I shall sleep better tonight.

But a sharp scream from the corridor, and a sound of running feet, startled her into an awareness of danger. She listened, motionless, ancient fears awakening. Silence. Opening her door cautiously, she saw light streaming from the Puseys' suite, and heard voices. Oh, God, she thought. A heart attack. And willed herself to take charge.

It was Jennifer's door that was open, and Jennifer herself, the straps of a satin nightgown slipping from her plump shoulders, laughing and uttering little moans, was poised on her bed, her legs drawn up. Her mother, in a pale pink silk kimono, stood in the doorway, her hand to her mouth. In the corner, crouching Mr Neville busied himself with a newspaper, then went to the window and flung something out.

'Quite safe now,' he pronounced. 'No more spiders.'

And he raised his eyes briefly to Edith.

Mrs Pusey came forward and laid a hand on his arm.

'How can we thank you?' she breathed. 'She's been terrified of spiders ever since she was tiny.'

But she was not tiny now, reflected Edith, whose mind had photographed an impression of Jennifer that it had not previously entertained. An odalisque, she thought. And the nightgown revealing quite a lot of very grown-up flesh.

In the corridor she waved goodnight to Mr Neville, whose secret smile was once again in place.

Later that night, Kiki, waking up from his long convalescence and feeling hungry, set up a plaint which continued until dawn. Drifting off into a final sleep, Edith thought she heard a door close.

6

'My dearest David,

'My cover has been blown, but of that more later.

'I am sorry not to have written for the last couple of days but the desert of the Hotel du Lac has begun to blossom like the rose with strange new relationships. I fear that Mrs Pusey and Jennifer can no longer count on me to listen to their shopping sagas (always a triumph: the last this, the finest that, whatever it may be) for I am going shopping myself, spurred into this unusual activity by my new friend Monica (Lady X) who is delighted to have an excuse to whizz off in a hired car to some little place she knows and to festoon me with an assortment of garments which are more to her taste than to mine. Indeed, it sometimes occurs to me that she and Mrs Pusey have far more in common with each other than either of them has with me, but for some reason they are not on good terms and use me as a buffer state. I am subject to a certain amount of balkanization. I can't say that any of this is deeply absorbing but I have bought a very beautiful blue silk dress and I think that you will like it. Monica says it makes me look years younger. I hate to think what I must have looked like when I first arrived.

'Monica herself is a stimulating if demanding companion. And I have found out why she is here. Monica has what is politely referred to as an eating problem: at least that is how she refers to it. One is always reading articles about this sort of thing in magazines. What it means in practice is that she messes her food around distastefully in the dining room, already slightly off-colour from acute and raging boredom, and ends up smuggling most of it down to Kiki, who is seated on her lap. In between meals she can be seen in a café near the station eating cakes. The story behind this is interesting. Her noble husband, in urgent need of an heir, has dispatched her here with instructions to get herself into working order; should this not come to pass, Monica will be given her cards and told to vacate the premises so that Sir John can make alternative arrangements. Naturally, she sulks. She eats cakes as others might go slumming. But she is very sad because she too longs for a child and I don't think she will ever have one. She is so beautiful, so thin, so over-bred. Her pelvis is like a wishbone!

'Our outings so far have followed a regular pattern. We wander through the town, while she gestures disdainfully at the goods, some of them very expensive, in the little shops. Then, when we arrive at Haffennegger's, she decides that she must have a cup of coffee, urgently. It is like being out with a child; she stops dead and refuses to go any further, and then Kiki starts up, and in we go. The cup of coffee escalates into several cakes, for she doesn't bother to pretend with me. She says she feels safe with me (who doesn't?) and the long rigmarole of her dilemma is poured forth once again. She hates and fears her husband, but only because he has not protected her, and she sees herself condemned to loneliness and exile. In this she is prescient. I see her, some years hence, a remittance woman, paid to live abroad, in such an hotel, in various Hotels du Lac, her beautiful face grown gaunt and scornful, her dog permanently under her arm. Her last weapon will be an unyielding snobbishness, which is already in evidence. She despises her husband's family as jumped-up ironmongers (I understand that one of his ancestors invented some small but crucial industrial implement at the beginning of the nineteenth century) and glorifies her own particularly feckless lot. She is what Iris Pusey would call a fortune-hunter. But it is unlikely that another fortune will be hers, and her fine hieratic face droops into sadness as she contemplates what she can see of her future.

'Naturally, all this is taking up much of the time that I intended to spend on my book, but I have been thinking that I might stay on a little longer. The weather is still beautiful.

'And I am getting some much needed exercise. A man here, a Mr Neville, who looks rather like that portrait of the Duke of Wellington that was stolen from the National Gallery some time ago, took me out on a very long walk yesterday . . .'

Edith laid down her pen, for it would have been inappropriate to continue. Coarse and mean thoughts hovered on the edges of her mind, waiting for a chance to take over. It was not, in fact, much to her taste to spend so much time talking about clothes or calculating other women's incomes or chances: such discussions had always seemed to her to be of intrinsically poor quality. And yet she was invariably drawn into such conversations, and although playing no active part, did not retire from them altogether untainted. Monica, for example. With Monica she entered a rueful world of defiance, of taunting, of teasing, of spoiling for a fight. The whole sorry business of baiting the sexual trap was uncovered by Monica's refusal to behave herself in a way becoming to a wife: by sheer effrontery she would damage her husband's pride, humble him into keeping her, or, if not, ruin his reputation. And although cast adrift while he pursued other interests, other plans, she was waiting for him, as one waits for an enemy; once they met, she would, by dint of insult and outrage, reawaken the fury that had once been between them. And until he came she would spend his money, waste his time, meditate her revenge. And, like the grand adventuress that she had once been, she would need a female attendant, a meek and complaisant foil, in whom she could confide, and whose opinion she could afford to discount.

And for Mrs Pusey, Edith reflected, she fulfilled the same function. Mrs Pusey and, by extension, Jennifer, were beginning to emerge in a rather harder light than had at first been apparent. Mrs Pusey had had the sort of success that Monica was scornful of achieving: bourgeois, luxurious, demonstrable. Mrs Pusey's references to her husband made Edith uneasy, perhaps because they appeared to be a function of Mrs Pusey's narcissism: Mr Pusey, who still had no name, would have remained without a profession or a home had these not been added by circumstantial evidence. His character, his tastes, even his looks were veiled in mystery. The manner of his departing this life was still obscure and undated, although Edith had learned to be wary of this final revelation, fearful of the bestowing of comfort and sympathy that this would inevitably call forth. I too have a past, she thought, with an uncharacteristic spurt of indignation. I too have had my deaths and my departures, some of them quite recent. But I have learned to shield them, to hide them from sight, to keep them at bay. To exhibit my wounds would, for me, denote an emotional incontinence of which I might later be ashamed.

Yet it was less Mrs Pusey's tranquil exhibitionism that worried Edith than the glimpses she had caught of a somewhat salacious mind. Mrs Pusey's disposition to flirt, even when there was no one around to flirt with, was, to Edith, somehow disturbing, although it was done with such lack of inhibition that it should have appeared harmless. On those rare occasions when Mrs Pusey was sitting alone, Edith had observed her in all sorts of attention-catching ploys, creating a small locus of busyness that inevitably invited someone to come to her aid. She would not be still or be quiet until she had captured the attention of whomever she judged to be necessary for her immediate purpose. And the enormous celebration of her own person, of her physical charm, so ruthlessly yet innocently set forth, was this altogether attractive in a woman of her age? This determination never to leave the field, not even for Jennifer, who appeared quite overshadowed, quite passive, in comparison with her mother's ardent eye, her cocked head, her passionate absorption in what to wear next. And that glimpse, that Edith had had, in her bedroom, of those exotic *déshabillés*, not all of them in the quietest of taste, did one laugh them off as a harmless indulgence, a simple love of adornment, of play? Which was surely, undoubtedly, what they were. Edith wondered, sensing ancient prejudices about to come to the surface. Her mother, Viennese Rosa, would have had no doubts at all. She would have taken one look at Mrs Pusey and laughed her grim laugh; she would have discerned at a glance the sort of temperament she most admired in a woman, a subject much debated with her sister and her cousin in those days when they discussed their conquests and their rivals just out of earshot of their mother and aunt. *Très portée sur la chose*, they would have agreed, in the atrociously accented French they used as a code. And Rosa would have curled her lip, not out of contempt, but out of vengeful regret for her own wasted years, which should have been filled with lovers and their intrigues but which had instead been monopolized by an increasingly mute husband and a silent child.

And Mrs Pusey hated Monica, in whom she sensed both opposition and failure. To Mrs Pusey, Monica was not merely a fortune-hunter but the sort of woman she, Mrs Pusey, should not be asked to admit into her presence. Those heights of scornful distinction, so effortlessly attained by Monica, were written off by Mrs Pusey as 'a front'. She did not say what lay behind the front. But she intimated that she knew.

The company of their own sex, Edith reflected, was what drove many women into marriage. So it had been with her. The meekness of her bowed head had failed to avert the confidences with which Penelope Milne daily sought to regale her and, even worse, the questions with which she felt authorized to confront her. Perfectly composed, tending her garden, writing, her face closed against pity, sympathy, curiosity, Edith kept silent and yearned for David.

They thought of her as an old maid, or at least a maiden lady. Randy spinsters of her acquaintance turned their eyes heavenward in despair when she answered, no, there was no one in her life, and never guessed that she lied. She lied well, unpretentiously: she sometimes thought that the time spent working out the plots of her novels had prepared her for this, her final adventure, her story come to life. David, she knew, lied not quite so well, even dropped hints to his wife, in one of those dangerous quarrels of theirs, that he might look elsewhere. His wife laughed scornfully, knowing him to be burdened with responsibilities – houses, children, professional standing – that he could not shed. His friends were indulgent towards him: he was attractive and they granted him licence to enjoy himself a little. But they suspected that he enjoyed himself with a succession of tough young secretaries, or with other men's wives. Never with her.

She knew his wife, of course, but contrived never to see her. Naturally reclusive, she found it unsurprising that people left her to her fate. There had once been a dinner party, which she had urged herself to attend as a matter of social duty, not knowing that he was to be there. Yet outside the drawing room, she had heard that triumphant laugh, and did not quite know, in that moment of confusion, whether it would take more courage to leave or to continue. In the event, her steps continued without her, and she found herself sitting, with a glass in her hand, and to all intents and purposes entirely normal. She behaved well, as she knew she was expected to behave: quietly, politely, venturing little. While she listened to the pleasant middle-aged man on her left (and as her hostess observed them with a pleased and proprietorial eye) she looked across the table and saw his wife, highly coloured, drinking rather a lot, argumentative. Sexy, she thought painfully. But discontented, nevertheless. Her neighbour held out a lighter for the cigarette she had taken and she turned to him with her usual grave smile. Later, as the evening was coming to an end, she saw that David was sitting with an arm on the back of his wife's chair, and that she, her eyes vague now, her face very pink, had become silent. She saw that they would make love that night and, getting up rather abruptly, thanked her hostess for a delightful evening.

'My dear, must you go? It's still quite early.'

'You must excuse me,' she said. 'I have something I rather want to finish . . .'

'Poor Edith. Burning the midnight oil. But such lovely books. We are all such fans, my dear. Now, how are you going to get home?'

Her neighbour offered his car and they left together. On the journey back from Chesham Place, she was rather silent. The man, who had been introduced as Geoffrey Long, was also silent, but she was vaguely aware of him as an affable and comforting presence. She told him not to get out of the car, but that he must come and have a drink with her one evening, exchanged telephone numbers with him, and waved him goodbye from her tiny front garden. Then she picked a sprig of lavender, crushed it between her fingers, and sniffed the aromatic leaf. And finally she went indoors. Oh David, David, she thought.

She knew that he was a man who could not deny himself anything. And that she had a part in his self-indulgence. That she must remember this.

When she telephoned her hostess the following morning, she learned that the evening had rather foundered after she had left. Or so she was given to believe. 'Priscilla *is* rather naughty. Poor David has his hands full at times. But of course they are absolutely devoted to each other.' She imagined scenes, conflagrations, accusations. But her hostess was saying, 'I'm so glad you got on with Geoffrey. He has been quite at a loss since his mother died. You must both come again, very soon.' But she thought that she would not go there again and, resolving to leave Geoffrey in those capable matchmaking hands, she said that she was going to disappear until the book was finished but would be in touch as soon as she was able to organize her time a little better. But that she would be so happy if her hostess would come to tea one day. The garden was looking so pretty.

That had been four years ago. And the disagreeable memory of David on that evening had been obliterated almost immediately after, when Penelope, who liked to rally her troops, whether they knew that they were hers or not, took Edith off to a sale at Simmonds'. They had found David with his warehouseman, Stanley: in their shirtsleeves, both were sitting in silent harmony on packing cases, while on a third packing case stood two mugs of tea and a plate of virulently coloured jam tarts. Hauling himself to his feet, David presented a smiling and attentive face, behind which Edith knew he was thinking of something entirely different, to Penelope, who was full of arch reproaches. Edith had watched her flush becomingly but talk too much as his eyes rested on her. 'Two-thirty, David,' Stanley had warned. And as Penelope turned to have a benevolent word with Stanley, Edith willed her features into neutral as David, shrugging into his jacket and questing her attention, allowed one eyelid to minimally fall. Thus, wordlessly, was an urgent meeting agreed upon.

When they next saw him, he was all business. Herded into rows of chairs, regressed to the obedience of childhood, they raised their eyes as to a pulpit. On the rostrum, David, gavel in hand, announced, 'Lot Five. *Time Revealing Truth.* Attributed to Francesco Furini. What am I bid?'

Edith, in her veal-coloured room in the Hotel du Lac, sat with her hands in her lap, wondering what she was doing there. And then remembered, and trembled. And thought with shame of her small injustices, of her unworthy thoughts towards those excellent women who had befriended her, and to whom she had revealed nothing. I have been too harsh on women, she thought, because I understand them better than I understand men. I know their watchfulness, their patience, their need to advertise themselves as successful. Their need never to admit to a failure. I know all that because I am one of them. I am harsh because I remember Mother and her unkindnesses, and because I am continually on the alert for more. But women are not all like Mother, and it is really stupid of me to imagine that they are. Edith, Father would have said, think a little. You have made a false equation.

She bent her head, overcome by a sense of unworthiness. I have taken the name of Virginia Woolf in vain, she thought.

She sat for a long time, then, humbly, got up, smoothed her hair, picked up her bag, and went down to tea.

The only person taking tea in the salon was Mme de Bonneuil, her old brown hands brushing the crumbs from the front of her dress. Edith smiled at her, and received a nod in return. The hotel had emptied since the weekend. The weather was still fine, but waning in conviction, as if its hold on heat and light were growing weaker. On the terrace, the mild sun had an opaque quality, dwindling into mist as the afternoon, shorter now, slowly disappeared. The warmth was humid, promising showers. Once again, the mountain was beginning to dissolve into the mist.

'There you are, dear,' said Mrs Pusey. 'You've been almost a stranger these past few days. Jennifer thought you had quite deserted us. Didn't you, darling?'

Jennifer raised her face from Mrs Pusey's abandoned copy of *The Sun at Midnight* and smiled, her beautiful digestive system momentarily at rest.

'Quite forgotten us, we thought,' she confirmed. 'Mummy was really upset.'

Murmuring disclaimers, Edith sank into her wicker chair, and asked them what they had done that day. And was rewarded by happy expressions, and a great deal of delightfully inconsequential information.

7

'One hardly notices the proximity of the glaciers,' said Edith appreciatively.

'No,' agreed Mr Neville. 'But then they are not all that close.'

They were seated outside a small restaurant under a vine-covered trellis, a bottle of yellow wine on the table between them. Shaded, they were able to look out across a small deserted square made brilliant by the sun of early afternoon. At this height the lake mists were no longer imaginable: half-tones and ambiguous gradations, gentle appreciations of mildness and warmth, were banished, relegated to invalid status, by the uncompromising clarity of this higher air. Up here the weather was both hot and cold, bright and dark: hot in the sun, cold in the shade, bright as they climbed, and dark as they had sat in the small deserted café-bar, resting, until Mr Neville had asked, 'Could you walk a little more?' and they had set off again until they reached the top of what seemed to Edith to be a mountain, although the golden fruit on the trees in the terraced orchards they had passed on their way rather gave the lie to this assumption. Now they sat after lunch, becalmed, the only two people contemplating these few square metres of flat cobbled ground, the only sounds the faint whine of a distant car and a mumble of music from a wireless deep in the recesses of the restaurant, perhaps from the kitchen, perhaps from the little sitting room at the back, where the owner might retire to read his newspaper before opening up again for dinner.

But who came here? In Edith's mind, Mrs Pusey and Monica and Mme de Bonneuil, the hotel itself with its elderly pianist and its dependable meals, seemed to be at the other end of the universe. The mild and careful creature that she had been on the lake shore had also disappeared, had dematerial-ized in the ascent to this upper air, and by a remote and almost crystalline process new components had formed, resulting in something harder, brighter, more decisive, re-alistic, able to savour enjoyment, even to expect it.

'Who comes here?' she asked.

'People like us,' he replied.

He was a man of few words, but those few words were judiciously selected, weighed for quality, and delivered with expertise. Edith, used to the ruminative monologues that most people consider to be adequate for the purposes of rational discourse, used, moreover, to concocting the cunning and even learned periods which the characters in her books so spon-taneously uttered, leaned back in her chair and smiled. The sensation of being entertained by words was one which she encountered all too rarely. People expect writers to entertain *them*, she reflected. They consider that writers should be gratified simply by performing their task to the audience's satisfaction. Like sycophants at court in the Middle Ages, dwarves, *jongleurs*. And what about *us*? Nobody thinks about entertaining *us*.

Mr Neville noticed the brief spasm of feeling that passed over Edith's face, and observed, 'You may feel better if you tell me about it.'

'Oh, do you think that is true?' she enquired, breathing rather hard. 'And even if it is, do you guarantee that the results will be immediately felt? Like those obscure advertise-ments for ointment that help you to "obtain relief". One is never quite sure from what,' she went on. 'Although there is sometimes a tiny drawing of a man, rather correctly dressed, with a hand pressed to the small of his back.'

Mr Neville smiled.

'I suppose it is the promise that counts,' Edith went on, a little wildly. 'Or perhaps just the offer. Anyway, I forget what I was talking about. You mustn't take any notice,' she added. 'Most of my life seems to go on at a subterranean level. And it is too nice a day to bother about all that,' Her face cleared. 'And I am having such a good time,' she said.

She did indeed look as if she might be, he thought. Her face had lost its habitual faintly sheep-like expression, its quest for approval or understanding, and had become amused, patrician. What on earth was she doing here, he wondered.

'What on earth are you doing here?' asked Edith.

He smiled again. 'Why shouldn't I be here?'

She gestured with upturned hands. 'Well, that hotel is hardly the place for you. It seems to be permanently reserved for women. And for a certain kind of woman. Cast-off or abandoned, paid to stay away, or to do harmless womanly things, like spending money on clothes. The very tenor of the conversation excludes men. You must be bored stiff.'

'You, I expect, have come here to finish a book,' he said pleasantly.

Her face clouded. 'That is quite right,' she said. And poured herself another glass of wine.

He affected not to notice this. 'Well, I am rather fond of the place. I came here once with my wife. And as I was at the conference in Geneva, and in no rush to get back, I thought I'd see if it were still the same. The weather was good, so I stayed on a little.'

'This conference,' she said. 'Forgive me, but I don't know what it was about.'

'Electronics. I have a rather sizeable electronics firm which is doing surprisingly well. In fact, it almost runs itself, thanks to my excellent second in command. I spend less and less time there, although I remain responsible for everything that goes on. But this way I can spend a good deal of time on my farm, and that is what I really prefer to do.'

'Where . . . ?'

'Near Marlborough.'

'And your wife,' she ventured. 'Did she not come with you?'

He adjusted the cuffs of his shirt. 'My wife left me three years ago,' he said. 'She ran away with a man ten years her junior, and despite everyone's predictions she is still radiantly happy.'

71

'Happy,' said Edith lingeringly. 'How marvellous! Oh, I'm so sorry. That was a tactless thing to say. You must think me very stupid.' She sighed. 'I am rather stupid, I fear. Out of phase with the world. People divide writers into two categories,' she went on, deeply embarrassed by his silence. 'Those who are preternaturally wise, and those who are preternaturally naive, as if they had no real experience to go on. I belong in the latter category,' she added, flushing at the truth of what she said. 'Like the Wild Boy of the Aveyron.' Her voice trailed away.

'Now you are looking unhappy,' he observed, after a short silence, during which he allowed her flush to deepen.

'Well, I think I am rather unhappy,' she said. 'And it does so disappoint me.'

'Do you think a lot about being happy?' he asked.

'I think about it all the time.'

'Then, if I may say so, you are wrong to do so. I dare say you are in love,' he said, punishing her for her earlier carelessness. Suddenly there was an antagonism between them, as he intended, for antagonism blunts despair. Edith raised eyes brilliant with anger, only to meet his implacable profile. He was apparently inspecting a butterfly, which had perched, fluttering, on the rim of one of the boxed geranium plants that marked the restaurant's modest perimeter.

'It is a great mistake,' he resumed, after a pause, 'to confuse happiness with one particular situation, one particular person. Since I freed myself from all that I have discovered the secret of contentment.'

'Pray tell me what it is,' she said, in a dry tone. 'I have always wanted to know.'

'It is simply this. Without a huge emotional investment, one can do whatever one pleases. One can take decisions, change one's mind, alter one's plans. There is none of the anxiety of waiting to see if that one other person has everything she desires, if she is discontented, upset, restless, bored. One can be as pleasant or as ruthless as one wants. If one is prepared to do the one thing one is drilled out of doing from earliest childhood – simply please oneself – there is no reason why one should ever be unhappy again.'

'Or, perhaps, entirely happy.'

'Edith, you are a romantic,' he said with a smile. 'I may call you Edith, I hope?'

She nodded. 'But why must I be called a romantic just because I don't see things the same way as you do?'

'Because you are misled by what you would like to believe. Haven't you learned that there is no such thing as complete harmony between two people, however much they profess to love one another? Haven't you realized how much time and speculation are wasted, how much endless mythological agonizing goes on, simply because they are out of phase? Haven't you seen how the light touch sometimes, nearly always, in fact, is more effective than the deepest passion?'

'Yes, I have seen that,' said Edith, sombre.

'Then, my dear, learn to use it. You have no idea how promising the world begins to look once you have decided to have it all for yourself. And how much healthier your decisions are once they become entirely selfish. It is the simplest thing in the world to decide what you want to do – or, rather, what you don't want to do – and just to act on that.'

'That is true of certain things,' said Edith. 'But not of others.'

'You must learn to discount the others. Within your own scope you can accomplish much more. You can be self-centred, and that is a marvellous lesson to learn. To assume your own centrality may mean an entirely new life.'

'But if you would prefer to share your life?' asked Edith. 'Supposing that you were a person who was simply bored with living their own life and wanted to live somebody else's. For the sheer pleasure of the novelty.'

'You cannot live someone else's life. You can only live your own. And remember, there are no punishments. Whatever they told you about unselfishness being good and wickedness being bad was entirely inaccurate. It is a lesson for serfs and it leads to resignation. And my policy, you may be surprised to hear, will ensure you any number of friends. People feel at home with low moral standards. It is scruples that put them off.'

Edith conceded his point with a judicious nod. This dangerous gospel, which she would have refuted at a lower level, seemed to accord with the wine, the brilliance of the sun, the headiness of the air. There was something wrong with it, she knew, but at the moment she was not interested in finding out what it was. More than the force of his argument, she was seduced by the power of his language, his unusual eloquence. And I thought him quiet, she marvelled.

'That is why I so much enjoy our dear Mrs Pusey,' Mr Neville continued. 'There is something quite heartening about her simple greed. And one is so happy to know that she has found the means of satisfying it. And, as you see, she is in good health and spirits: altruism has not interfered with her digestion, conscience has not stopped her sleeping at nights, and she enjoys every minute of her existence.'

'Yes, but I doubt if all this is good for Jennifer,' said Edith. 'Or good enough, I should say. At her age there should be more to life than buying clothes.'

'Jennifer,' said Mr Neville, with his fine smile. 'I have no doubt that in her own way Jennifer is a chip off the old block.'

She leaned back in her chair and raised her face to the sun, mildly intoxicated, not so much by the wine as by the scope of this important argument. Seduced, also, by the possibility that she might please herself, simply by wishing it so. As a devil's advocate Mr Neville was faultless. And yet, she knew, there was a flaw in his reasoning, just as there was a flaw in his ability to feel. Sitting up straight, she returned to the attack.

'This life you advocate,' she queried, 'with its low moral standards. Can you recommend it? For others, I mean.'

Mr Neville's smile deepened. 'I daresay my wife could. And

that is what you are getting at, isn't it? Do I tolerate low moral standards in other people?'

Edith nodded.

He took a sip of his wine.

'I have come to understand them very well,' he replied.

Well done, thought Edith. That was a faultless performance. He knew what I was thinking and he gave me an answer. Not a satisfactory answer, but an honest one. And in its own way, elegant. I suppose Mr Neville is what was once called a man of quality. He conducts himself altogether gracefully. He is well turned out, she thought, surveying the panama hat and the linen jacket. He is even good-looking: an eighteenth-century face, fine, reticent, full-lipped, with a faint bluish gleam of beard just visible beneath the healthy skin. A heartless man, I think. Furiously intelligent. Suitable. Oh David, David.

Mr Neville, noting the minute alteration in her attention to him, leaned over the table.

'You are wrong to think that you cannot live without love, Edith.'

'No, I am not wrong,' she said, slowly. 'I cannot live without it. Oh, I do not mean that I go into a decline, develop odd symptoms, become a caricature. I mean something far more serious than that. I mean that I cannot live *well* without it. I cannot think or act or speak or write or even dream with any kind of energy in the absence of love. I feel excluded from the living world. I become cold, fish-like, immobile. I implode. My idea of absolute happiness is to sit in a hot garden all day, reading, or writing, utterly safe in the knowledge that the person I love will come home to me in the evening. Every evening.'

'You are a romantic, Edith,' repeated Mr Neville, with a smile.

'It is you who are wrong,' she replied. 'I have been listening to that particular accusation for most of my life. I am not a romantic. I am a domestic animal. I do not sigh and yearn for extravagant displays of passion, for the grand affair, the

75

world well lost for love. I know all that, and know that it leaves you lonely. No, what I crave is the simplicity of routine. An evening walk, arm in arm, in fine weather. A game of cards. Time for idle talk. Preparing a meal together.'

'Putting the cat out?' suggested Mr Neville.

Edith gave him a glance of pure dislike.

'That's better,' he said.

'Well, you obviously find this very amusing,' she said. 'Clearly they order things better in Swindon, or wherever it was that you . . . I'm sorry. I shouldn't have said that. It was extremely rude of me. How dreadfully . . .'.

He poured her out another glass of wine.

'You are a good woman,' he said. 'That is all too obvious.'

'How is it obvious?' she asked.

'Good women always think it is their fault when someone else is being offensive. Bad women never take the blame for anything.'

Edith, breathing hard, wondered if she were drunk or simply rendered incautious by the novelty of this conversation.

'I should like some coffee,' she announced, with what she hoped was Nietzschean directness. 'No, on second thoughts, I should like some tea. I should like a pot of very strong tea.'

Mr Neville glanced at his watch. 'Yes,' he said. 'It is getting on. We should be making a move soon. When you have had your tea,' he added.

Edith drank her tea fiercely, unaware that the exertion of thinking, so remote, so unusual in her present circumstances, had brought colour to her cheeks and added brightness to her eyes. Her hair, slipping from its usual tight control, lay untidily on her neck, and with a gesture of impatience she removed the last securing hairpins, raked her fingers through it, and let it fall about her face. Mr Neville, appraising her with faintly pursed lips, nodded.

'Let me tell you what you need, Edith,' he said.

Not again, she thought. I have just told you what I need and I know what that is better than you do.

'Yes, I know you think you know better than I do,' he said, as her head shot up in alarm. 'But you are wrong. You do not need more love. You need less. Love has not done you much good, Edith. Love has made you secretive, self-effacing, perhaps dishonest?'

She nodded.

'Love has brought you to the Hotel du Lac, out of season, to sit with the other women, and talk about clothes. Is that what you want?'

'No,' she said. 'No.'

'No,' he went on. 'You are a clever woman, too clever not to know what you are missing. Those tiny domestic pleasures, those card games you talk about, they would soon pall.'

'No,' she repeated. 'Never.'

'Yes. Oh, your romanticism might keep rueful thoughts at bay for a time, but the thoughts would win out. And then you would discover that you had a lot in common with all the other discontented women, and you'd start to see a lot of sense in the feminist position, and you'd refuse to read anything but women's novels . . .'.

'I write them,' she reminded him.

'Not that sort,' he said. 'You write about love. And you will never write anything different, I suspect, until you begin to take a harder look at yourself.'

Edith felt the hairs on the back of her neck begin to crepitate. She had told herself as much, many times, but had been able to dismiss her own verdict. Now she recognized the voice of authority, as if she had heard an illness confirmed, although she had almost succeeded in persuading herself that she was only imagining the symptoms.

'Do you really want to spend the rest of your life talking to aggrieved women about your womb?' he went on, inexorably.

'I really don't think I have much of a womb to talk about,' she said, with an unhappy laugh.

'Oh, you would become gloomy about it in due course. In any event, I doubt if anyone's bears close inspection.'

'Tell me,' said Edith, after a pause, 'you don't by any chance do psychiatry as a sideline, do you? Since the electronics industry leaves you so much spare time?'

'What you need, Edith, is not love. What you need is a social position. What you need is marriage.'

'I know,' she said.

'And once you are married, you can behave as badly as everybody else. Worse, given your unused capacity.'

'The relief,' she agreed.

'And you will be popular with one and all, and have so much more to talk about. And never have to wait by the telephone again.'

Edith stood up. 'It's getting cold,' she said. 'Shall we go?'

She strode on ahead of him. That last remark was regrettable, she thought. Vulgar. And he knows where to plant the knife. Yes, writing in my room leaves me free to be telephoned; who knows what might happen if I went out? And suddenly she longed for such solitude, like a child who has become overexcited at a party, and who should have been taken home, by a prudent nurse, some time ago.

'I am sorry,' he said, catching her up. 'Please. I don't want to pry. I know nothing about you. You are an excellent woman, and I have offended you. Please forgive me.'

'You are sadistic,' she said, pleasantly.

He inclined his head. 'So my wife used to tell me.'

'And how do you know that my capacity for bad behaviour is unused? That is a mild but definite form of sexual insult, you know. Less well publicized than bottom-pinching or harassment at work, but one with which quite a lot of women are familiar.'

'If your capacity for bad behaviour were being properly used, you would not be moping around in that cardigan.'

Edith shot ahead, furious. To contain her anger – for she could not find her way down to the lake unaided – she tried various distancing procedures, familiar to her from long use. The most productive was to convert the incident into a scene in one of her novels. 'The evening came on stealthily,' she muttered to herself. 'The sun, a glowing ball . . .'. It was no good. She turned round, searching for him, listening for the steps which should be following her and were not, and feeling suddenly alone on this hillside, in the cold. She shivered and wrapped her arms around herself.

'I hate you,' she shouted, hopefully.

A steady crunch of gravel announced the reappearance of Mr Neville. When his face came into focus, Edith saw that it was wearing its usual smile, intensified.

'You are coming along very well,' he said, taking her arm.

'You know,' she said, after ten minutes of silent descent. 'I find that smile of yours just the faintest bit unamiable.'

His smile broadened. 'When you get to know me better,' he remarked, 'you will realize just how unamiable it really is.'

8

'Dearest David,

'Astounding news! Mrs Pusey, that pinnacle of feminine chic, that arbiter of taste, that relentless seeker after luxury goods, that charmer of multitudes, is *seventy-nine*! I know this because she had a birthday two days ago and we were all invited to celebrate it. Premonitory rumours that something was afoot had reached me earlier in the day; as I was going out along the corridor I heard cries of delight and surprise emanating from the Puseys' suite, while a veritable miasma of scent (a different sort) seemed to billow out almost to the head of the stairs. While I stood on the steps outside the hotel, I could see a boy emerging from a van with an arrangement of flowers which looked positively bridal; I thought no more about it, although had I worked it out I would have realized that nobody would have sent flowers to Monica or Mme de Bonneuil or myself, and that only left the Puseys. Of course, Jennifer might have a boyfriend somewhere, and the higher reason suggests that she must have, but somehow it seems unlikely. I think she is the sort of girl who will never leave her mother. I have met many such daughters. Penelope, you might be surprised to know, has refused offers of marriage because in her opinion few of the men she meets come up to Mother's exacting standards, of which I have heard so much. Penelope quotes Mother as the final authority on every subject, and sometimes I envy her this certainty, this piety. I wish that I had had a mother who handed down maxims on tablets of stone, and who was never without a wise saw or a modern instance. I never knew my poor mother to do much more than bark with derision. And yet I think of her as my poor mother. As I grow older myself I perceive her sadness, her bewilderment that life had taken such a turn, her loneliness. She bequeathed to me her own cloud of unknowing. She comforted herself, that harsh disappointed woman, by reading love stories, simple romances with happy endings. Perhaps that is why I write them. In her last months, she lay in bed, wearing the silk peignoir that my father bought her on their honeymoon in Venice, not caring, perhaps not noticing, that the lace was torn, the pale blue faded to grey, and when she raised her eyes from her book, her eyes too were faded from blue to grey, and full of dreams, longings, disenchantment. My mother's fantasies, which remained unchanged all her life, taught me about reality. And although I keep reality in the forefront of my mind, and refer to it with grim constancy, I sometimes wonder if it serves me any better than it served my mother.

'But all this is by the way. I went out for the day and when I turned up for dinner that evening all was revealed. The dining room had emptied after the bustle of the weekend and was reduced to a paucity of numbers which spelled out "end of season" for anyone who had an instinct for such things. Even the waiters seemed to have given up and could be seen talking among themselves. Monica fed her first course to Kiki quite openly and nobody seemed to care. Mme de Bonneuil, who eats very quickly, sits silently between courses, smoothing the tablecloth with her hands. I was three quarters of the way through my sweetbreads when I was aware of a slight commotion in the doorway, and there I beheld Mrs Pusey being led in, laughing and protesting, by M. Huber. It was clear that this was no ordinary occasion. Not only was her table decked with flowers (the ones I had seen delivered that morning) but Mrs Pusey had scaled heights of dressing up that put the rest of us to shame. To be quite truthful, I did not think that she had quite brought it off. Her midnight blue lace was surmounted by a sort of spangled jacket, obviously extremely expensive; this in its turn was enlivened by several strings of beads, pearls, gold chains, and even a rather beautiful lapis lazuli pendant. Her hair had been re-gilded, and her nails were flawlessly pink. I have to say that she looked quite splendid, in a baroque sort of fashion. By that I mean that either she appeared out of context or the rest of us did. It seemed to me that the verdict was in the balance only for a brief moment. After that, it began, imperceptibly, to go in Mrs Pusey's direction. Of course she willed it so, but there is always some sort of consensus in these matters. And in that crucial moment the consensus was somehow secured. Waiters darted to pull out her chair; menus were flourished in front of her; champagne produced for her inspection. Mme de Bonneuil watched all this quite impassively. Monica rolled her eyes heavenwards.

'You must understand that we were not prepared for any of this. We were all in our mid-week, fairly subdued, evening wear, saving the one "best" dress for Friday, and the second "best" dress for Saturday, and something agreeable but appropriately understated for Sunday. Inmates of institutions quickly learn the rules. I was wearing that green dress which you have always disliked, safe in the knowledge that you would not be here to dislike it. Within minutes of Mrs Pusey's arrival, I could see why you disliked it, and resolved never to wear it again. Monica was particularly put out because although she always looks very beautiful, on this particular evening she had managed not to: perhaps her black dress made her look too thin and also too pale. The shadows cast by the ivory knobs of her cheekbones made her seem ill, doomed. Mme de Bonneuil was also in black, but then she always is; I think she has two or at the most three black dresses of an ageless, shapeless, timeless, and indeed fashionless type into which she changes every evening. I would be quite unable to describe these garments to you in detail, largely because they contain no detail. But I have to say that she always looks entirely correct. She looks as a woman of her age should look, and I dare say the same could be said of Monica and myself.

'Once these reflections had died down I realized that Jennifer too had made an effort. Indeed it was Monica's rather too eloquent grimaces that stimulated me into casting a glance in Jennifer's direction. What I saw was somewhat of an eye-opener, if you will permit the vulgarity. To celebrate her mother's birthday, Jennifer had attired herself in pink harem pants, teamed, as they say in the fashion mags, with an off the shoulder blouse. She too had been to the hairdresser, who had done her proud; shining blonde waves, redeemed from their earlier artlessness, had been drawn back into a kind of top-knot, leaving two short ringlets bobbing in front of her ears. I had not noticed how plump she was. They both are, really. But they carry it so well that one hardly notices. Anyway, they made a brave sight. Slightly bizarre, perhaps, but that may have been because the rest of us were so subdued. The thought of all the effort they had put into their preparations made me feel quite faint with exhaustion. And they are on holiday! And there was practically nobody there to take any notice of them! Except for us, of course, but we could hardly be thought adequate to the occasion, having no visible passports to this garden of earthly delights. I think there was a moment in which we felt this, and it cast a shadow over the proceedings.

'But Mrs Pusey, for whom I was beginning to feel something like pity, horror, compassion, is an old hand at this game. Glasses of champagne were delivered to Monica and Mme de Bonneuil and myself, and then we all had to drink her health, and there was a certain amount of bobbing up and down and nods and becks and wreathèd smiles, most of which were cast about by Mrs Pusey herself. Monica and Mme de Bonneuil, more stoical about this sort of celebration than I am, drank stolidly, although Mme de Bonneuil raised her glass in a rather charming slow gesture before draining it. And then, when it seemed as if the entertainment were over, and the event duly noted, Alain and another boy in a white coat wheeled in a trolley on which there reposed a cake of such splendour that even Mme de Bonneuil looked impressed. M. Huber was quite beside himself with pride. Mrs Pusey laughed, and hid her face in her hands, and even applied one of her elaborate lace hand-kerchiefs to the corner of one eye, as more champagne was poured into her glass. Jennifer expertly supervised the cutting and distribution of the cake, despatching waiters to all our tables with chocolate-laden plates. This time we had to raise forks in acknowledgement. It was absolutely delicious.

'And of course we could hardly leave Mrs Pusey on her own after dinner. For the first time in living memory, all the guests took their coffee together in the salon. It was not an altogether homogeneous assembly, but Mrs Pusey, her lipstick slightly smudged in the general effervescence, appeared not to mind. Mme de Bonneuil, who could hear nothing, and who was used to doing her duty, or perhaps simply to doing what was expected of her, sat it out gamely, smiling from time to time in the direction of Mrs Pusey or nodding kindly at Jennifer. She struck me, on this occasion, as a creature of some nobility, for she was far from home, far from genuine reasons for celebration and, I should judge, a stranger to such elaborate games of make-believe. Monica, though occasionally winking at me when she thought no one was looking, joined in with rather more enthusiasm than I would previously have given her credit for; indeed, she showed how well she could play the social game when she tried, although there was a satirical intention hovering over her every remark. When she went a little too far in her general teasing, I noticed that she became the object of Jennifer's level scrutiny. But Monica's genuine interest was aroused, as I knew it would be, must be, by Mrs Pusey's clothes, and soon they were on almost equal terms as they exchanged the names and addresses of dressmakers: both hit on the same one, although this was not immediately evident, since Mrs Pusey described her as "my little woman", while to Monica she was "a chum of mine". For a harmonious moment peace was restored, as they engaged in a cross-fire of brand-names that spanned the entire continent. Gucci and Hermès, Chanel and Jean Muir, The White House and Old England, were just a few that I recognized. At this point Mme de Bonneuil, who had perhaps endured as much as she thought was expected of her, heaved herself out of her chair, raised her stick in farewell to Mrs Pusey, and rocked her way out of the salon. "Poor old soul," said Mrs Pusey, in what seemed to me to be a loud voice, although of course Mme de Bonneuil could not hear.

'We kept it going, though realistically the party should have broken up at this stage. You know how difficult it is to sustain an occasion when all the attention is being sucked one way: again I noticed the Puseys' curious refusal of mutuality. Behind their extreme pleasantness there lies something entrenched, non-negotiable, as if they can really take no one seriously but themselves. As if they feel sorry for anyone who is denied the possibility of being a Pusey. And this, of course, is, by definition, everyone. I wonder if Jennifer is ever to marry. On which outsider will descend the supreme accolade of becoming an insider? How will he be recognized? He will have to present impeccable credentials: wealth equal to theirs, or, if possible, superior, a suitably elevated style of living, an ideally situated residence, and what Mrs Pusey refers to as "position". All these attributes will come before his physical appearance, for Jennifer might be led astray by that into making a hasty judgment. My feeling is that the chosen one will be agreeably but perhaps not emphatically masculine; he will be courtly and not too young and very patient and totally indulgent. He will have to be all of these things because if he is to be a match for Mrs Pusey's vigilance he will have to spend a great deal of time with her. With them both. In fact I see Jennifer's married life as being an extension of her present one; simply, there will be three of them instead of two. The only rite of passage will be the wedding, and as this will be seen primarily as the pretext for buying more clothes its ultimate significance will be occluded. This man, Jennifer's husband, will occupy a position equidistant between the two of them, on call in both directions. He will perforce be the man of the family, but he will not be a Pusey. And in any event, were they not perfectly happy before he came along? Were not their standards of excellence confined to themselves? How could he possibly justify any suggestion of change?

'I have no feeling that Mrs Pusey is ever going to die. With some people (I know them well), the shadow of their death precedes them; they lose hope, appetite, viability. They feel the meaning of their lives draining away, and they recognize that they have lost, or never attained, their heart's desire, and they give up. In the eyes of such people one reads dreadful recognition, the ultimate self-knowledge: I have not lived enough and it is too late to redeem myself. But Mrs Pusey's beautiful materiality would seem to preclude such ideas, thoughts, premonitions, whatever one cares to call them. Mrs Pusey, having secured for herself the good things in life, has no intention of letting them go, and why should she? She knew from the outset what some unfortunates never learn; she knew that the best is there to be taken, although there may not be enough to go round. One should congratulate her on her perspicacity. Anything else one feels is probably no more or no less than sour grapes.

'"But it's your birthday," cried Monica, who was evidently following the same train of thought as I was. "Now which one, I wonder?" This Mrs Pusey tried not to hear. (In fact, at this point it occurred to me that she might be a bit deaf. Almost certainly, now I come to think of it. Those monologues, which take no account of anyone else, which are impermeable to anyone else's opinion – perhaps these are the characteristic of someone who cannot, for reasons of vanity, admit to deafness.) "Darling," she said to Jennifer. "Do go and ask Philip to join us. He knows we don't stand on ceremony." At which Jennifer, her face once more rosy and blank, trotted over to Mr Neville, who had somehow concealed himself while these celebrations were taking place but who was now obliged to surrender his plans for the evening and join us.

'Monica, however, was not to be deflected. "Come along, now," she insisted, in a playful tone which nevertheless brooked no argument. "I'll bet you just can't face the fact of being sixty. Is that it? Well, you don't look it." Mrs Pusey laughed. "Age is relative," she parried. "You're as old as you feel. And sometimes I feel as if I'm still a girl." Her voice shaded off into artless wonder as she pronounced these words: to us, her audience, she seemed to be hesitating on the brink of womanhood, amazed at the cornucopia of riches which the world had to offer her.

'"But you've got Jennifer." said Monica, rather unkindly, I thought, and so, evidently, did Jennifer, who scrutinized her with that same level look, a look which made her seem much older than ... Than what? Perhaps the champagne was making me feel tired, perhaps I was tired already, but suddenly I had the uncanny feeling that this was all for show, that everything was a pretence, that this had been a dinner of masks, that no one was ever, ever going to tell the truth again. I wanted you then, David, very much. But you were not there. Only Mr Neville was there, enjoying himself hugely. Mr Neville, I should explain, is a connoisseur of the fantastic, an intellectual voluptuary of the highest order.

'The sad fact is that Mrs Pusey, although still game, suddenly looked rather old. But when, after long and sustained courtesies on the part of Mr Neville, she finally revealed that she was seventy-nine, we were all genuinely astonished. Calculations flashed through our minds; each of us knew exactly what the others were thinking. If Mrs Pusey admits to seventy-nine, then Jennifer must be about my age. Mine and Monica's. And that is what she is. Jennifer, like me, is thirty-nine, although her curious combination of plump body and expressionless face makes her seem no older than fourteen. For what Jennifer insistently expresses, now that I come to think of it, is latency. She has the unsettling presence, or possibly the equally unsettling absence, of many adolescents; her apparently uninformed voluptuousness would be almost shocking if it were not cancelled by her daughterly obedience. Jennifer is blatantly wholesome, seemly, innocent. Yet in comparison, I, who am none of these things, feel like her maiden aunt.

'It was then that Mrs Pusey, coaxed on by the attentive Neville, told us how the early years of her marriage were overshadowed by the completely inexplicable absence of children. Here another snowy handkerchief was produced from her bag, shaken out, and applied to the corner of her lips. "No matter how hard we tried," she said, "nothing seemed to work." She sighed reminiscently. This remark hung rather heavily in the atmosphere; Monica brooded, while I wished that I had left earlier, with Mme de Bonneuil. Then, after twelve years of selfless and dedicated "trying", Mrs Pusey's efforts were rewarded, and lo and behold, there was Jennifer. "My husband always wanted a little girl." Here she turned to Jennifer, who flashed her an altogether expected smile and lovingly held out her hand. Thus encouraged, Mrs Pusey went on to regale us with anecdotes of Jennifer's early years. Needless to say, these were all they would have hoped for, although she was outrageously spoiled. "Well, when you've waited so long, you tend to give them everything they want, don't you? And my husband couldn't bear to see her in tears. It upset him dreadfully. Iris, he used to say, let her have the best. I'll leave you a blank cheque. And so we did, and she's none the worse for a bit of spoiling, are you, darling?" Again, the smile, the outstretched hand. And certainly Jennifer's glossy health would seem a more than adequate repayment for such efforts, on which, for some obscure reason, Mrs Pusey had to be congratulated all over again. I have to tell you, David, that among other things, Jennifer had a pony called Twiglet. And then we had the full recital again: Haslemere, Head Office, and how she has everything delivered.'

Edith laid down her pen. This letter would have to be finished later, and even possibly revised. Unsound elements seemed to have crept into her narrative; she was aware of exceeding her brief. And was then aware of the restrictions that that brief implied: to amuse, to divert, to relax – these had been her functions, and indeed her dedicated aim. But something had gone wrong or was slipping out of control. What had been undertaken as an exercise in entertainment – for had not the situation seemed appropriate, tailor-made, for such an exercise? – had somehow accumulated elements of introspection, of criticism, even of bitterness. 'Well, darling, what news from Cranford?' David used to say, stretching out his long arm to gather her to him as they sat on her big sofa. And that had always been her cue to present him with her gentle observations, always skilfully edited, and to watch the lines of fatigue on his lean and foxy face dissolve into a smile. For that is how he saw me, she thought, and out of love for him that is how I tried to be.

But now, possibly because of the champagne, she felt unsettled, wary. There seemed to be no immediate reason for this except fatigue, stretched nerves. The evening, of course, had gone on far too long after an extraordinary day. At some point, Monica had started to tell her story to Mrs Pusey, who listened with avid interest masked by an air of solicitous condescension. There seemed to be no means of escape. Jennifer, one ankle balanced on the opposite knee, this attitude permitted by the entirely modest amplitude of her harem pants, yet still managing to be both childish and inappropriate, seemed to have absented herself once more behind her docile face. She lay back in her chair, toying with her curls, her eyes watching from under half-closed lids; from her teeth a tiny thread of saliva hung glistening. Edith swallowed invisible yawns. She was aware that even Mr Neville was mildly inattentive, although his habitual courtesy of expression gave nothing away.

They had still been there at midnight. Monica, once launched, was not to be side-tracked, and cigarette after cigarette was smoked. And Mrs Pusey had nothing really helpful to offer in the way of advice; indeed, memories of her own term of trial, so successfully concluded, inclined her only to bracing clichés, which had not gone down too well. Monica's face had drooped into its habitual lines of discontent, and the evening had ended on a distinctly less harmonious note than that on which it had started, and, at one point, had bid fair to continue. At least Kiki was absent, shut into

Monica's bathroom again by Alain after yet another misdemeanour. M. Huber, somewhat disappointed in his role of master of ceremonies, had nevertheless stayed downstairs, hoping for words of appreciation. But these were not forthcoming. It seemed as if everyone were too tired to redeem the situation, and when Mr Neville offered his arm to Mrs Pusey she was only too happy to accept it. It took a little longer than usual for her to lever herself out of her chair, but finally she had left, leaning on Mr Neville, with Jennifer bringing up the rear.

Edith, reaching the haven of her room, closing the door behind her, tried to discover the reason for her low spirits, which seemed intricately bound up with the events of this evening, and the thoughts it had provoked. Was it that she was simply a stranger to the very act of celebration? Mrs Pusey's birthday, Jennifer's imagined wedding, had seemed to her so very much more three-dimensional than anything she could remember in her own life. For her birthdays in her parents' house, Edith herself had made the cake and her father had brought it in, ceremoniously, with the coffee. Those occasions had been brief and timid excursions into family life as she had supposed they might ideally live it; her mother was stimulated into reminiscences of the coffee houses of her youth, and had talked vividly and amusingly, before falling once again into the sorrow of reminiscence. By that time the coffee had been drunk and on the plate the cake lay in ruins, and when Edith carried it back into the kitchen, her birthday had been over. And there had never been any mention of weddings.

And now, paradoxically, in the blessed silence and dimness of her room, Edith felt her own fatigue dissolve, and the underlying unease, of which she had been intermittently aware during the writing of her letter, began to stir, to increase, to take over. And at this very late hour, she felt her heart beat, and her reason, that controlling element, to fragment, as hidden areas, dangerous shoals, erupted into her consciousness. The careful pretence of her days here, the almost successful tenor of this artificial and meaningless life which had been decreed for her own good by others who had no real understanding of what her own good was, suddenly appeared to her in all their futility. Perhaps the champagne, the cake, the celebration, had eroded the barriers of her mind, trailing sly and unwelcome associations, making a nonsense of those careful arrangements she had worked out for herself, banishing amusement, returning her to seriousness and to painful reflection, demanding an accounting. She had thought that by consenting to this tiny exile she was clearing the decks, wiping the slate, and that she would be allowed to return, suitably chastened, in due course, to resume her life. 'I am clearing the decks, Edith,' she remembered her father saying, as he tore up the papers on his desk. 'Just clearing the decks.' He had smiled, but his eyes were full of sad knowledge. He had known that nothing would be the same for him again, that his stay in the hospital was not to be the brief interlude he had bracingly told her mother it would be. And he had not come home. And maybe I shall not go home, she thought, her heart breaking with sorrow. And beneath the sorrow she felt vividly unsafe, as she did when she saw that the plot of a novel would finally resolve itself, and how this might be brought about.

Sitting alone in the silence, she bowed her head and passed scrupulously in review the events that had brought her, out of season, to the Hotel du Lac.

9

On the day of her wedding Edith had woken earlier than usual, her senses alerted by the quality of the light, which was hard, white and uneasy, harbouring surprises of an unpleasant nature, far removed from the mature sunshine on which she had been counting. She took the weather as an omen, and her abrupt awakening as a sign, though of what she could not say or even think. More to the point, as she passed her dressing table she caught sight of her face and was shocked to see it so pale and drawn. I am no longer young, she thought; this is my last chance. Penelope is right. It is high time I forgot my hopes, the hopes I was born with, and faced reality. I shall never have that for which I long with my inmost heart. How could I? It is too late. But there are all the comforts of what is called maturity: pleasant companionship, comfort, proper holidays. It is a reasonable prospect. And I was always a reasonable woman, she thought. We are all agreed on that.

And Geoffrey Long, that kind man who had been produced for her at that not too far distant dinner party, and who had been so lonely since his mother died: what more excellent guarantee could anyone produce of a safe and sensible future? Only a very innocent man, she thought, could play the traditional suitor so openly, and how impressed everyone had been, principally Penelope, but in the end even Edith herself, by his devotion, his generosity, his endless flowers, his fussy care, and finally his mother's gloomy opal ring. And he had offered her a complete life, a new home to move into, new friends, even a cottage in the country, luxuries which she would never have thought to procure for herself. And he was a personable man, if a little old-fashioned in his views: he did not, for example, approve of women working, and he teased her about the amount of time she gave to her books. And there was something so agreeably straightforward, even comic, about his courtship. And everyone said how good he had been to his mother. Everyone said how lucky his wife would be. Everyone said how lucky Edith was. Penelope said it with that faintly nettled air that implied that she herself would have been a more worthy recipient. And Edith was constantly reminded of her good fortune. And, really, there was no need to disclaim any of this. She was lucky. I am lucky, she reminded herself, looking at that drawn face in the glass of her dressing table.

She made a pot of very strong tea, and while she was waiting for it to draw she opened the kitchen door to inspect her garden. But there was a small and niggling wind which blew a tiny shower of dust around her ankles, and the door kept swinging backwards and forwards, interrupting the curious light, bringing intimations of cloud, although there was no cloud, and a cessation of things to be taken for granted. Like this little house, so long her private domain, a shell for writing in, for sleeping in, silent and sunny in the deserted afternoons, before the children came home from school, and turned in at other gateways. Those becalmed afternoons, when the strength and heat of the sun on the window at her back merely drove her relentless typing fingers onward as if they had a life of their own. And the ensuing exhaustion, always signalled by an alteration in the light, which returned her to herself and to her tense back and shoulders and her slight cramp, and an awareness of untidy hair and smudged hands, and with this awareness a disgust, as if something orgiastic had taken place, while the children were coming home from school. Then, leaving that room, she would go down to the kitchen and open the back door, sniffing the heavenly, the normal, air, while waiting for her kettle to boil. And would take her tea to her plain little white bathroom, where she would wash away the day's fatigue and its residue, and hang up the simple cotton dress she wore for working in, as if only some unassuming garment were appropriate for her daily task – that illicit manufacture of a substance not needed for survival. And in her bedroom, a cool room which got the morning sun only, and then for a brief period, she would dress herself carefully and brush her hair, as she had been taught to do, a long time ago, and pin it up with her usual unthinking expertise, and when she had judged herself, gravely, in the mirror, to be presentable, she would go downstairs, pour herself another cup of tea, and at last feel ready for the garden.

She would miss the garden most, she thought, although she was not really a gardener. Most of the work was done by a taciturn and alarmingly pale boy from the greengrocer's; what he lacked in words he made up for in his passion for plants and the assiduity with which he cared for them. He came three times a week, in his lunch hour, and she would leave his lunch on the kitchen table: she tried to tempt his appetite, worried about his white face, and although he longed for a cheese roll and a bottle of beer, he swallowed her careful delicacies, sensing that this was important to her, and taking it seriously. 'I'm off then,' he would call up the stairs. 'Might look in Sunday.' 'All right, Terry,' she would call back. 'The money's on the dresser.' For the money seemed to them both a separate issue, hardly connected with the loving work of housekeeping to which they both, in their different ways, applied themselves.

The garden was only truly hers in the very early morning and in the evening, after her day's work, when she simply sat on a rather uncomfortable wrought-iron bench – a kind gift from Geoffrey who had laughed at her old spreading creaking wicker chair – and watched the sun dip below the hedge and welcomed an increase in the sharpness of the scents. At this time, she knew, her neighbour's child, a child of heartbreaking beauty whose happiness and simplicity were already threatened by a crippling speech defect, would come out to see if she were there (but she was always there) and would slip through the hedge to say goodnight. And Edith would watch her wrestling with the words, her thin little body juddering with the effort to unlock them, and she would smile and nod as if the words were perfectly intelligible, and would put her hands to the child's jerking head to still it, and would whisper, 'Good night, my little love. Sleep well.' And would kiss the child, now calm, and send her off to bed.

The evenings were less interesting. A visit to Penelope to hear about the day's events, a small meal, half of which Terry had had for his lunch, the plants to be watered, and then bed, very early. Sometimes it was still light when she went to bed, but as the light was of such very great interest to her she would put down her book just to watch it fade, and change colour, and finally become opaque and uninteresting. Then it was time to sleep. Her bed was white and plain and not quite big enough. Geoffrey Long, a sturdy man, had wincingly, but with his usual good nature, remarked on this more than once. As had Penelope, whose own bed would have accommodated four adults and which, when not in use, was heaped with all manner of delicate little pillows covered in materials which proclaimed to the world at large, 'I am a woman of exceptional femininity.' Some women raise altars to themselves, thought Edith. And they are right to do so. Although I doubt if I could carry it off.

In any event, the marital bed in Montagu Square, where Geoffrey had formerly lived with his mother, had already been installed, and soon she would take her place within the confines of a handsome bedroom, the colours of which she secretly found a little too insistent. She had chosen them herself but had, fatally, perhaps, invoked the aid of Penelope who had guided her expertly through a selection of department stores, while discoursing on the ways to please a man. 'It's no good being wishy-washy, Edith,' she had said, several times. 'A man can't feel at ease in a cell. You have to recognize his needs.' Edith, feeling faint in this airless world and apologetic because she found so little to arouse her enthusiasm, and because Penelope seemed so much more involved in the enterprise than she was herself, succumbed at last to her persuasions, and also to the terribly thin face of the poor salesman, whose lunch hour they were monopolizing, and chose a counterpane of dull marigold, with expensive marigold

95

coloured towels to hang in their dark green marble bathroom, and some thick satin-bound blankets the colour of cinnamon. They were new and handsome, but it seemed to her that they absorbed the light and were stuffily authoritative. She could not see herself ever repairing to this bedroom after a day's writing, or taking a nap on the splendid cane-headed bed. And she had noticed precious few children in Montagu Square, and there was no garden, so that her day would have an entirely different pattern when her writing time was over. But then she would not be writing. Perhaps she would never write again. She would have that life that she supposed other women have: shopping, cooking, arranging dinner parties, meeting friends for lunch. All those worldly acquaintances who had been so kind with their invitations to little gatherings and whom she had hitherto repaid only with a desire that they should see her garden. I have not paid my dues, she said to herself, on a day when she had looked with timid pleasure at her new and spacious kitchen. I must have seemed like a foundling to them. That will have to change.

And it had changed. No one had been hurt. On the contrary, everyone was delighted. David had laughed at her new recklessness and had teased her with an unknown lover. 'You must be in love,' he had said. And she, not daring to break that unwritten contract between them, had not said what she wanted to say, and had missed her chance for ever. So that when he had taken her hand surreptitiously one day at a private view to which she had gone with Penelope, and she had guided his thumb to her third finger where he had felt the rim of Geoffrey's mother's ugly ring, he had stiffened, but had said nothing. What was there to say? There had been no promises. And later that evening, on their last meeting, he had pressed his face into her neck and mumbled, 'Do you mean it?' And she had meant it, because sometimes he stayed away too long. And because he had not dissuaded her. But a month later, on her wedding morning, she was still standing in her kitchen, thinking of all the things she had not yet said to him.

The sound of a key in the lock had made her start. Her irregular cleaning lady, Mrs Dempster, pink-cheeked, brilliantly coiffed, generously sober, looked at her with amazement. 'Not dressed yet?' she marvelled. 'I hope you've had your bath, at least.'

'Why?' asked Edith. 'What time is it?'

'It's ten o'clock,' articulated Mrs Dempster, slowly, as if to a child. 'Ten o'clock. You're getting married at twelve, remember? And in case you're wondering what I'm doing here, well, there's the little matter of the caterers to supervise. You remember that, I suppose. You're coming back here for a buffet lunch, in case it slipped your mind, before you sail off into the blue.'

She breathed hard as she donned her spotless overall, as if the very prospect of a marriage unsettled her nerves, which were notoriously unpredictable. Men were her downfall, she had confided, over many a cup of coffee; very little work was done. Edith suspected that Penelope got more out of her, but then, she conceded, Penelope had more to offer in the way of confidences. Penelope and Mrs Dempster, in fact, had something in common; their entire conversation revolved around the subject of men, whom they seemed to like and to dislike in equal measure. So that when Mrs Dempster said, 'Come on, love. You have your bath and I'll make you a nice cup of coffee to have while you're dressing,' Edith had turned away, tears pricking her eyes. The kindness of people, she thought. Their unexpected kindness.

Lying in the bath, she could hear the house reverberating to Mrs Dempster's voice commanding a troop of men. Cases of champagne were dumped, rather heavily, somewhere beneath her. The promised cup of coffee had been postponed, in the greater excitement of supervising the arrangements: the little house shuddered with the inroads of florists and of the team of girls who would now turn the kitchen into their own domain as they manufactured the asparagus rolls and the mushroom vol-au-vents and the tiny cheese beignets and the iced fingers of orange cake, and the Nesselrode pudding. 'Pudding, Edith? You must be mad,' said Penelope. 'My mother loved it,' countered Edith, and thought, privately, that her mother would have considered this a puny alliance. Girls with high but severe voices could be heard demanding more vases, or calling from the back to the front of the house, 'Sarah! Do get a move on! We've got to be out of here by eleven-thirty if we're going to do Tregunter Road. Oh, coffee! You angel, Mrs Dempster. Sarah! Coffee!' And there was suddenly a complete cessation of activity, as if they had decided to call the whole thing off. But when Edith went back to her bedroom, she found a cup of coffee on her dressing table and in the saucer a couple of biscuits, which Mrs Dempster must have brought with her, for Edith did not remember buying any.

She dressed in the fine stockings and the beautiful grey satin slip. She had rejected Penelope's offer to oversee her wedding clothes, and had gone, on a series of unaccustomed buses, to an elderly Polish dressmaker in Ealing with some fine blue-grey material in a mixture of silk and wool. And here she was, dressed in a very creditable Chanel copy, the jacket bound with a dark blue and white silk braid. Mme Wienawska had also made her a plain round-necked blouse, which she wore with her Aunt Anna's pearls, her only dowry, the only token of her family's presence. Her shoes were blue and white, and, she thought, a little too high in the heel, and she carried her white gloves. She had refused to wear a hat, but had twisted her hair up a little higher than usual, and when she looked in the glass she was pleased with herself. She looked elegant, controlled. Grown-up, she thought. At last.

A faint sensation of pleasure, the first she had felt that day, began to suffuse her, and her face wore a welcoming and naive smile as she descended the staircase. Sarah and her friends (Kate? Belinda?) had no time for her, and Mrs Dempster was engaged in meaningful conversation with Penelope at the kitchen table. Penelope, Edith was interested to see, was wearing an obviously expensive dress of printed silk and an enormous red straw hat, the brim of which curved round her head and skimmed down the side of her face nearly to her shoulder. A strong smell of scent emanated from her many pleats and folds, and Mother's famous diamond earrings were in place, touched from time to time by fingers with long scarlet nails. This outfit had Mrs Dempster's full approval; it was indeed radiantly nuptial, although it formed a strange contrast to the hefty denimed haunches of the girls intently rolling almond biscuits round the handles of wooden spoons. Whatever Penelope had been discussing with Mrs Dempster was instantly abandoned and Edith found herself the object of their stern and almost disembodied scrutiny. Who would carry the day? she wondered, with almost equally disembodied interest. Penelope, with her emphatic knowledge of what a man really likes, or me, blessed only by the genius of my Polish seamstress? If there were a man here we could re-enact the Judgment of Paris. Except that if that man were Geoffrey (and now it could be no one else) he would find something acceptably gallant to say to all of us.

The silence was broken by one of the girls who were turning out her wedding breakfast with surprising speed. 'Oh, jolly nice,' she said. 'Look, would you mind moving, only we want to be out of here pretty sharpish and we'd like to clear up. Good luck and all that,' she added.

So Edith had been reduced to walking round the garden, while Penelope and Mrs Dempster continued to oversee the girls in the kitchen and to hope that Edith realized how lucky she was, working on the mutual understanding that, in her case, such luck was not to be taken for granted and was not even all that deserved. 'In a dream, half the time,' observed Mrs Dempster, 'making up those stories of hers. I sometimes wonder if she knows what it's all about.' Penelope laughed, and Edith, seeing this through the open kitchen door, wondered if she might be allowed in to share the joke. 'My dear, I'm the one with all the stories,' she was in time to hear Penelope say. 'I wonder she doesn't put me in a book.'

I have, thought Edith. You did not recognize yourself.

But she was tired and chilled and even rather hungry. She felt as if she were emerging slowly from some debilitating illness and might at any moment be prone to headaches and fits of tears. It seemed to her that she should be wearing something warm and shabby – a dressing gown would be ideal – and sipping a nourishing milky drink. She felt acutely alone, and thought that perhaps many brides felt the same. But surely few brides were left to sit in the drawing room, on their best behaviour, occasionally getting up to look out of the window to see if the cars were arriving. And when the first huge gleaming car did arrive, was it the duty of the bride to walk back to the kitchen, now hot and friendly, and announce, 'Penelope, your car is here'? For it had been decided, Edith could not now remember by whom, that Penelope, as matron of honour, should be the first to arrive at the Registry Office and should there join forces with Geoffrey and his best man, who was a larger but sleepier version of Geoffrey himself. And that they would thus be ready to welcome Edith, who would arrive fifteen minutes later, in the second car, alone. Mrs Dempster, at her own request, would stay behind, using Edith's bedroom in order to change into her own highly distinctive wedding outfit and would be there to welcome them home and do the honours of the buffet.

After Penelope had been persuaded to depart, and had taken her time over it, enjoying the impassive gazes of a small group of crisp-eating children waiting outside the house, there was a moment of calm. The girls trooped out, already intent on the time and calculating the distance to Tregunter Road. Mrs Dempster could be heard upstairs, running water for a bath. Edith stood by the window. And then, all too soon, it was her turn.

As her own car drew slowly away, Edith fell into a somewhat regressive state of mind. Details of her little house front struck her as if she were seeing them for the first time. It should have been painted, she thought, and then, I really ought to have it done. And then she noticed the extraordinary charm of the shops which she passed unseeingly every day: the funeral parlour, the chemist, the newsagent, with his discreet display of adult magazines, most of which had covers which showed girls bending over and winking through their legs, the betting shop with its mass of torn paper tickets littering the pavement outside. As the car rolled her on towards her destiny, she noted, with deep nostalgia, the Cypriot green-grocer emerging from the depths of his shop with a bucket of water; this was flung in a wide arc over the pavement, causing Edith to feel a shock of pleasure. She saw the hospital and the young men in white coats charging up the steps, and the adventure playground, and the day nursery, and the place that sold plants, and one or two pubs, and a rather nice dress shop. And then she saw the Registry Office and a small crowd chatting on the pavement in front of the entrance. Like a visitor from another planet, she saw her publisher and her agent and her poor father's crazy vegetarian cousin and several of her friends and quite a few neighbours. And she saw Penelope, animated, her red hat attracting the attention of one or two of the photographers, conversing with the best man and with Geoffrey. And then she saw Geoffrey. And then she saw, in a flash, but for all time, the totality of his mouse-like seemliness.

Leaning forward, in a condition of extreme calm, she said to the driver, 'Would you take me on a little further, please? I've changed my mind.'

'Certainly, Madam,' he replied, thinking, from her modest demeanour, that she was one of the guests. 'Where would you like to go?'

'Perhaps round the park?' she suggested.

As the car proceeded smoothly past the Registry Office, Edith saw, as if in a still photograph, Penelope and Geoffrey, staring, their mouths open in horror. Then the scene became slightly more animated, as the crowd began to straggle down the steps, reminding her of a sequence in some early master-piece of the cinema, now preserved as archive material. She felt like a spectator at some epic occurrence, was prepared for shots to ring out, fatalities to occur. But soon, amazingly soon, she had left them all behind, and as if to signal her escape the sun came out and blazed hectically, and with the full heat of a late false summer behind it, over Sloane Square. And then they were proceeding at a steady and stately pace through the park; Edith opened the window and breathed with ecstasy the fresher air, giving delighted attention to the little boys playing football, and the heavy girls thumping up and down on horseback, and the tourists peering at their maps and, presumably, asking the way to Harrods.

'Once more,' she begged. But now her exaltation was beginning to fade as the thought of the consequences waiting to be faced confronted her. By now everybody would be back at the house, Geoffrey seated in the drawing room, possibly with his head in his hands, Mrs Dempster grimly demanding what she was to do about the food, Penelope master-minding the entire proceedings. This time she noted that the leaves were turning, and the sky becoming overcast again, and that she felt very cold. And, regrettably, still hungry.

After that, it had all been terrible. She found her little house vibrant with indignation, although she was glad to see her publisher and one or two of her older friends sipping champagne in the garden. She crept upstairs to her bedroom but found it littered with Mrs Dempster's clothes and smelling of Mrs Dempster's scent. Downstairs she could hear Penelope saying, 'Do help yourselves to everything. At least we can offer you some food. I cannot think where Edith has got to; she must have been taken ill.' At which Edith had sighed and made her way timidly down the stairs, very much aware of the indelicacy of her appearing at all.

She made her way straight to the drawing room and put her hand on Geoffrey's shoulder. 'Geoffrey,' she said, 'I'm sorry.' He looked up, and with momentous dignity removed her hand. 'I have nothing more to say to you, Edith,' he pronounced. 'You have made me look a laughing stock.'

'I think, Geoffrey, that you will find that it is I who am the laughing stock.'

This he ignored. 'I am only grateful that my poor Mother did not live to see this day.'

They both looked at the opal ring, which Edith removed and handed to him. Then she said, 'Goodbye, Geoffrey,' and left the room.

'I shall be in the garden, Penelope,' she announced, thus provoking a renewed wave of scandalized excitement. 'I just want to have a word with Harold and Mary.' And, taking a glass of champagne, she moved into the garden, exchanged a few pleasant words, but no explanation, with her agent, and sat there until she was sure that everyone had left.

She was condemned out of hand, of course. For what seemed like hours she listened to Penelope and Mrs Dempster discoursing on her moral turpitude, her childishness, her lack of dignity, trust, loyalty, and decent feminine sensibility. She then heard them tell her that she had had her last chance. That there was no future for her in that line, whatever she may think. That they wondered how she could hold up her head. That the best thing she could do would be to go away until she had come to her senses and could made decent reparation to society for the outrage she had committed. She had listened to all this in silence, her head bowed, until finally the voices had stopped, and the steps had retreated and the front door banged, and she was alone. She waited for five cautious minutes, then made her way indoors to the telephone and dialled a number.

'Stanley,' she said. 'Is David there?'

'Doing a sale outside Worcester,' was the reply. 'Anyone could have done it. I don't know why he went.'

'Could you get in touch with him for me? Could you ask him to come round this evening? As soon as possible? It's Edith, by the way.'

'Didn't you get married then?' asked Stanley, unsurprised.

'No,' she said. 'I changed my mind.'

She went upstairs to her bedroom, now restored to her, but still smelling of scent, opened the window, and changed out of her beautiful suit into a blue cotton dress. She sat on the bed for perhaps half an hour, contemplating her disgrace. Then, moving to the window to close it, for it was now evening and chilly, she was in time to see Geoffrey emerging from Penelope's house and looking decidedly more cheerful. Gone out to book a table, she supposed.

Two hours later she sat in the dark, waiting for the sound of David's car. Her mind was quite empty, but she was filled with longing, a longing which she now perceived to be fatal. For this misdemeanour could hardly be overlooked, would inevitably cause a whole chain reaction of amusement, caution, withdrawal. Quarrels can be made up; embarrassment can never quite be forgotten. Edith foresaw, sadly, that she would become an embarrassment.

Yet David, when he came, took her in his arms and said nothing. When he released her, he held her at arm's length and looked at her. She saw strain in his face, and tiredness, and knew that she had caused both. And something else. He looked rueful, wary. The situation was too complicated, too loaded, for the unwritten contract between them to bear. For they were reasonable people, and no one was to be hurt, not even with words. Above all, not with words. And so, with her last ounce of energy, and that was rapidly disappearing, she made a joke of it. An accident of timing, she said. Poor Geoffrey had been a stand-in; what she really needed was a holiday. Clearly she was not cut out to be a married lady. But they might as well finish the champagne. And, in the end, after watching a lugu-brious film on television, he was quite relaxed, and they were loving again. But she noticed with sorrow, after waving him goodbye, that he had not touched the plate of little delicacies she had salvaged for him from the wedding breakfast.

She had sat out the next few days, waiting to hear from him, but plans had been made in her name, and when the telephone rang it was Penelope, with the name and address of this excellent hotel, and information about flights, and what to pack. It had seemed to suit everyone that she should disappear, and to make sure that she did so, Penelope monitored her every movement. She was allowed out to have lunch with her agent and to leave him her address, for it was now grimly assumed that henceforth she would have to live on her wits, or at least by her pen. And on that last grey day, summer quite gone, she had found herself, unresisting, in Penelope's car, on the way to the airport. Mrs Dempster had promised to come in the following day to give the house a final overhaul, and to return the key to Penelope. She could not see her way clear, she explained, to coming back. She was funny like that. Sensitive. Edith would have to make other arrangements.

But as the car had drawn away, Edith had been comforted to see Terry, paler then ever, making his steady way along the pavement with a box full of bedding plants. He had raised his free hand, with his spare key in it, when he saw her, and she had waved back. At least, she thought, the garden will be cared for.

10

Edith, her head aching with the follies and perils of prolonged reminiscence, had finally made her way to bed at an advanced hour, when the entire hotel was silent and no cars could be heard on the road that ran along the shore of the lake. Sleep had come suddenly, like an anaesthetic: total blackness. When she opened her eyes, it was to the same unvariegated grey that had greeted her on the afternoon of her arrival. She had forgotten to pull the curtains and the daylight was all around her. Alarmed, as if she had been absent from this scene for some time, during which unknown events might have taken place, she sat up and reached for her watch. It was eight o'clock, a reasonable hour at which to awake if one's day had no structure, but for Edith, who was accustomed to begin her writing very early, sometimes even before the milk or the newspaper had been delivered, guiltily and unconscionably late.

She rang for her breakfast, and bathed and dressed hastily, anxious to remove the traces of the disarray into which the previous night's thoughts had plunged her. Then she went to the window and stepped out on to the little balcony: the unexpected cold made her shiver. One could hardly say that it was winter, but it seemed as though it were no longer autumn. The trees, rigid in the windless air, were beginning to show the skeletons of their shapes; leaves no longer fell but lay curled, sapless, on the fading grass. The sounds of morning were cautious and intermittent, as if few people were left. Down below, at the entrance, a man in a jersey was polishing his car. Edith recognized it as the car that came regularly to take Mrs Pusey and Jennifer on their day's outing. One of the chambermaids emerged and exchanged some words, which Edith could not hear, with the driver. Yawning, the woman rubbed her cheek, and then stood irresolutely, looking out over the lake. All the signs were of impending closure, of relaxation.

No one would come now. In the grey distance Edith could barely discern the outline of the mountain.

Hungry, for sadness affected her that way, Edith turned back into her room and wondered why her breakfast had not appeared. She moved to the bed and picked up the telephone, mildly surprised at having to ask twice, for this had never happened before. But as she put the receiver to her ear she could only hear a prolonged buzzing at the other end, as if there were no one to take her call, and after a minute or two she replaced it, thinking that some of the staff must have been laid off, and that she might as well make her way into town and have some coffee there. In any event, she was anxious to escape, for the room had become a prison, witness as it was to all her past misdemeanours, and she had no heart for the pleasantries she might be called upon to exchange with the Puseys, or with Monica, or indeed with Mr Neville.

While she was changing into her walking shoes she became aware of a sudden babble of voices from the corridor, a door opened and then firmly shut, even banged, and a rising sound of altercation, dominated by a boy's hoarse voice. Mystified, she moved out into the corridor where noises of distress could be heard coming from the direction of the Puseys' suite and where she saw M. Huber and his son-in-law conferring, apparently on a plan of action, before turning in at Mrs Pusey's room. Both wore such inscrutable expressions that Edith surmised that the previous evening's entertainment had proved too much for Mrs Pusey, that some sort of accident or illness had occurred, and that terrible and expert hotel arrangements were being made to remove her to hospital. She retreated into her room and tried to compose herself. She felt as if grief and terror had been unleashed by her long night of introspection and that she must now be called to account whenever and wherever damage might be done and atonement might be made. Then, composing herself with an effort, she opened her door once more and went along to the Puseys' little salon; here she found herself the last to arrive on a scene which already contained Monica, Alain, M. Huber, and M. Huber's son-in-law. Penetrating into the room she saw Mrs Pusey lying on a chaise-longue, her hand to her breast, but nevertheless fully made-up and wearing her pink silk kimono. Mrs Pusey's eyes were closed and as Edith, shocked, wondered how she could best be of use, she saw M. Huber advance and take Mrs Pusey's hand. Leaning over her he murmured something and began to pat her wrist. The boy, Alain, was red-faced and near to tears; he stood stiffly, staring ahead, as if facing a court martial.

'Mrs Pusey,' said Edith, breaking the silence. 'Are you all right? What has happened?'

Mrs Pusey's eyes opened. 'Edith,' she said. 'So good of you to come.' She seemed distant, admonitory. 'Go in and sit with Jennifer, would you?'

With fear clutching her stomach, still innocent of breakfast, Edith went into Jennifer's room prepared to find a scene of infraction or outrage, with Jennifer ill or possibly deranged. What she saw was indeed Jennifer, but Jennifer propped up in bed, her face moody and flushed, her mouth set in a pout, her plump shoulders emerging from the slipping décolletage of a virginal but very slightly transparent lawn nightgown.

'Are you all right?' asked Edith again. 'Has anything happened?'

Jennifer shot her a glance. 'I'm all right,' she said, without further explanation.

'Can I do anything?' asked Edith, puzzled, for Jennifer quite clearly was all right.

'Well, I could do with some more coffee. This lot's gone cold.' She gestured to her breakfast tray, awakening in Edith fresh pangs of hunger.

'Just coffee?' she asked. 'You don't want a doctor or anything?'

'Good God, no. Just look after Mummy, would you? She's a bit upset.'

She seemed gloomy, and curiously unhelpful. Sulky, Edith

thought. And why so inactive? If her mother is unwell she should be with her. What on earth is all this to do with me?

She backed out of Jennifer's bedroom into the salon, where she found M. Huber remonstrating with Alain, while Mrs Pusey closed her eyes again, and M. Huber's son-in-law attempted, unsuccessfully, to restore calm. Monica was leaning against the door, her eyebrows raised, her mouth wry. All looked up as Edith appeared, ready to receive a message.

'Jennifer would like some hot coffee,' she said.

M. Huber's son-in-law went out into the corridor and snapped his fingers to someone waiting outside. M. Huber, deprived of this steadying influence, took Alain by the arm and shook him. '*Imbécile*,' he pronounced, between shakes. '*Imbécile*.'

Alain, his composure foundering, breached his own code of honour and blurted, '*Mais je n'ai rien fait! Je n'ai rien fait.*'

'*Imbécile*,' repeated M. Huber, now breathless. '*Madame*,' cried the boy, appealing to Edith. '*Dîtes-leur. Je n'ai rien fait.*'

'Would somebody tell me ...' began Edith, but these cautious words were too much for Alain and he broke away, just as the tears, long held back, spurted from his eyes, and before they could catch him he was out and running down the corridor, shouting 'Maryvonne! Maryvonne!' A door opened, and Maryvonne's frightened blonde head emerged. Blunderingly Alain ran towards her; her arm went round him, her head came close to his, and both disappeared down the stairs.

In Mrs Pusey's salon there was a silence, as if nobody knew what to do next. This silence was broken by the arrival of more coffee, at which time Monica, M. Huber and his son-in-law chose to leave, assuring Mrs Pusey that she had only to call if she needed anything. Edith made as if to join them, for clearly there was no illness, no infraction, nothing that could not wait until later. As she moved towards the door, Mrs Pusey made a weak gesture with her hand.

'Don't go, Edith,' she murmured. 'I'm still in shock.'

But as Edith watched her sit up and pour her coffee, she seemed, perhaps by virtue of this sociable action, to recover both her energy and her presence of mind. 'Take some in to Jennifer, would you, dear?' she asked, as if this were the most normal request in the world. 'I've sent her back to bed. All this upset. I thought we'd spend the morning resting. Then perhaps we'll get up for lunch. Or have it sent up here. I doubt if I shall be hungry.' She gave a tremulous sigh.

'Mrs Pusey, can you tell me what happened?' asked Edith, taking the fragrant and still so elusive cup of coffee destined for Jennifer. 'What is the matter with Jennifer? She seems perfectly all right to me. And why was M. Huber shaking poor Alain?'

'Poor Alain?' Mrs Pusey bridled. 'I like that. Poor Alain indeed.'

'But what did he do?' pursued Edith.

'Nothing,' said Mrs Pusey grimly, applying a handkerchief to the corners of her mouth. 'But who knows what he might have done?'

'I'm sorry,' said Edith. 'But I still don't know what has happened.'

'I slept badly,' said Mrs Pusey. 'I didn't get off until dawn. And then I was awoken by a noise. A door. Someone in Jennifer's room, I thought. My heart was in my mouth. If anything happened to her . . .'

'But nothing has happened to her,' said Edith gently.

'So I struggled up,' Mrs Pusey went on, taking no notice. 'I rang the bell. And I forced myself to go through, although I was shaking. I may have screamed. But she was all right, thank Heaven.' She wiped her mouth again.

'In fact, all that you heard was Alain taking in her breakfast,' said Edith. 'It is quite late, you know. You overslept and you woke suddenly. And you're quite all right now.'

Mrs Pusey poured herself another cup of coffee. 'Oh, of course, I came back here and pulled myself together, but it's the shock, Edith, the shock.' She did indeed seem agitated. 'And of course when Jennifer sees me upset she gets upset. I've told her not to get up,' she repeated. 'And I've told Mr Huber to put one of the maids on this floor. I'm not having that boy hanging around. I never liked him. His eyes are too small.'

Edith, who had been standing all this time, turned away from Mrs Pusey's couch and walked to the window. In her mind was a picture of Jennifer, sitting up in bed, her shoulders bare, her nightgown just vestigially slipping down. And then of Alain, breaking into a boy's ugly tears, and escaping down the corridor. And she remembered – but had she really heard it? – the sound of that door opening and closing. I wonder, she thought. I wonder.

She leaned her head momentarily against the cold glass of the window, leaving Mrs Pusey to finish her coffee. She tried to quell the seed of disapproval, of discomfort, that she felt might grow rather rapidly if not subjected to some control. Mrs Pusey is afraid, she reminded herself. For Mrs Pusey, any alteration in the status quo must inspire fear. She is old and vain and she cannot afford to feel afraid; it is essential for her to deflect her feelings onto someone else. They will all get over it; it will all be forgotten by this evening. But from now on, I think I shall make myself less available to the Puseys. After all, we have nothing in common.

She turned back in time to see Mrs Pusey delicately spooning the remains of the melted sugar from her emptied coffee cup. 'Perhaps you had better rest,' said Edith, rather more firmly than before. 'I should have a quiet day, if I were you. I'm sure all this can be forgotten quite easily.'

'Of course, he'll have to go,' Mrs Pusey went on. 'I shall speak to Mr Huber. There'll be no difficulties there, I can assure you. When I think of all the years I've been coming here! What my husband would have done I dare not think.' She breathed heavily, her hand once more to her chest. 'Yes, you go, dear, if you must. I know you want to go out. Such a walker. Just send Mr Huber up to me, would you, when you go downstairs?'

Edith closed the door quietly behind her. There was no one

in the corridor, no one on the stairs. Baths were running, vacuum cleaners being plied; the voices of the maids could be heard raised in discussion in one of the bedrooms. Passing the desk on her way out, she could see M. Huber and his son-in-law in intimate conversation, for once on excellent terms, their expressions adult, expert, wry. Nodding slightly, she walked straight past them and out through the revolving door. The cold air, now damp with the mist that was creeping in from the lake, made her shiver; she felt ill-equipped and out of sorts, but also instinctively averse to going back to the hotel for a warmer sweater. Coffee, she thought. And then a very long walk, and if possible lunch somewhere far away. I need not come back until this evening. In fact, it might be better if I kept out of everybody's way for a while. My patience with this little comedy is wearing a bit thin.

Pacing through the dead leaves, her hands plunged into the pockets of her cardigan, Edith felt eddies of disturbance from the morning's incident beginning to widen until they encompassed both her present circumstances and her more long-lasting predicament. Although the scene around her remained grey and chill, although the rare faces she encountered were closed against the unpromising weather, cautiously husbanding smiles and greetings until they might be more propitiously offered, with a safer hope of return, the small change of the day, even the impersonal sadness of this late season, seemed to her more salutary than the enclosed world of the hotel, with its smells of food and scent, its notice taken of favours granted or withdrawn, its long memories, and its sharp eyes, and its contractual arrangements to behave agreeably and as if nothing untoward could ever happen. It is because we are so many women, thought Edith, to whom the scene in Mrs Pusey's salon returned most painfully. A stupid little misunderstanding like that, if it was a misunderstanding, will go on being mined for hurt feelings, and will be exploited for one reason or another, while the rest of us will use it as a subject for conversation from here to eternity or until one of us leaves. God knows there is little enough else to talk about. But it made Mrs Pusey feel unsteady, and she is not used to that: she must talk it all away. She must distance it until her momentary weakness is clearly seen as being *someone else's fault*, and in that way the shadow of her mortality will be exorcized. She is not used to fear. She has been protected for so long that she cannot understand why she should be vulnerable. In fact she cannot understand why anybody should be vulnerable. That may be why she is so ruthless. She has been allowed to proceed to her present monstrous cosiness through sheer ignorance of the world. Yet when her defences are breached she reveals an altogether shrewd grasp of the tactics needed to repair them. Poor Alain, she thought, pacing along unseeingly, her head down. Yet why poor? He is probably laughing with Maryvonne at this very minute. It is all over and forgotten. Yet that is not quite right either, she thought, mildly tormented.

When her agitation died down sufficiently to allow her hunger to gain the upper hand once more, she turned into Haffenegger's, where she saw Monica already seated at a table and wolfing down a large slice of chocolate cake, deaf to Kiki's tiny pleas, and so intent on her plate that she could barely spare the time to raise a fork briefly in Edith's direction. Edith sat down near the door, drank two cups of coffee and ate a brioche; then, sighing, but because she too was lonely, she moved over to Monica, whose face was now grim and wreathed in cigarette smoke. They exchanged a steady look, nodding slightly.

'Well,' said Edith, with an attempt at cheerfulness. 'Any plans for today?'

'Do me a favour, Edith,' replied the other. 'I am not feeling particularly bright this morning and I do not have any plans. I never have any plans. I should have thought that was fairly obvious by now. I thought you were supposed to be a writer. Aren't you supposed to be good at observing human nature, or something? I only ask because you sometimes strike me as being a bit thick.' She stabbed her cigarette end into an ashtray and left it there to smoulder.

'I'm sorry,' said Edith, removing the ashtray. 'I don't feel particularly bright myself. And I didn't say I was any good at observing human nature. Why should I be? It seems to me that what I see is so very different from what I think that I don't trust my judgment any more. I'm just as disappointed as you are, I can assure you. Perhaps more,' she added, sadly.

They brooded in the smoky atmosphere. The windows were once more steamed up, the coat rack laden with the heavier garments of the late season; desultory sounds of muted conversation or of spoons tapped against cups or glasses to summon the waitress brought in their wake the realization that for some people this was home, that for such people Haffenegger's was simply a part of their daily round, their domestic routine, and that these people would go back, not to hotels, but to real houses, complete with books and television sets and kitchens, where they could sit peacefully or read or cook, where they could open the back door and throw crumbs out for the birds, and where their children and grandchildren could visit them at weekends. With aching throat Edith thought of her little house, shut up and desolate, and to which no one came. I must go home, she thought. And then, no, not yet, not while this sadness is on me. I will wait until I am more buoyant. I will get through somehow.

'Monica,' she said suddenly. 'Are you fond of your mother?'

'Yes, of course,' said the other, surprised. 'Though she's mad as a hatter. Small doses are quite sufficient. But, yes, of course, I adore her. Why?'

'I just occasionally get the feeling that I must be an unnatural daughter. My mother is dead and yet I find that I hardly ever think of her. And when I do, it is with a wistfulness that I never felt for her in real life. Pain. And I think that that is probably how she thought of me. But I only miss her in the sense that I wish she could have lived long enough to see that

I am like her in the only way she valued: we both preferred men to women.'

'Well, who doesn't?' said Monica, her brows arching to their fullest extent.

'It occurs to me – and possibly that silly incident this morning may have brought it home to me – that some women close ranks because they hate men and fear them. Oh, I know that this is obvious. What I'm really trying to say is that I dread such women's attempts to recruit me, to make me their accomplice. I'm not talking about the feminists. I can understand their position, although I'm not all that sympathetic to it. I'm talking about the ultra-feminine. I'm talking about the complacent consumers of men with their complicated but unwritten rules of what is due to them. Treats. Indulgences. Privileges. The right to make illogical fusses. The cult of themselves. Such women strike me as dishonourable. And terrifying. I think perhaps that men are an easier target. I think perhaps the feminists should take a fresh look at the situation.'

She stopped. What she was trying to say, although deeply felt, did not make much sense. It is I who am at fault, she thought. It is because I am so meek that people fail to notice my demands. Or it is, even more simply, that I fail to make them. So much for honour. Honour is what David would call a busted flush. And nobody seems to notice when it has gone.

'Above my head, I'm afraid,' said Monica, putting an end to her meditations. 'Anyway, you've got nothing to worry about, I should have thought. Our Mr Neville has taken quite a shine to you.'

'Oh, nonsense,' protested Edith. 'Just because we went for a walk . . .'

'Well, he hasn't gone for a walk with anyone else, has he? No, I reckon that if you played your cards right you could have him. And he's worth quite a bit, I gather. Trade, of course.' This statement was accompanied by a particularly disdainful exhalation of smoke. It was not clear how Monica had gathered that Mr Neville was worth quite a bit; what was clear was that Edith had not.

'Monica,' said Edith wearily. 'That is not what I meant at all. I am not after Mr Neville or his money. I earn my own money. Money is what you earn when you grow up. I loathe the idea of women prospecting in this way.'

'I can't see anything wrong with it,' retorted Monica, but without much heat. 'Men do it too,' she added, after a pause. They both drooped, their spirits low, dimly aware that any remark would fail to elicit the expected response. They sat moodily, contemplating their exile. After a few moments, Monica signalled to the waitress and ordered cakes for both of them. Why not? thought Edith. At least we needn't go back for lunch. And I am not hungry anyway.

They ate in silence, feeling exposed and guilty, graceless, as women eating alone without enjoyment do feel. The sweetness burst in Edith's mouth, cloying quickly; sated, she passed her plate over to Monica, who fed the remaining crumbs to Kiki.

'I wonder that dog isn't monstrously fat,' remarked Edith, 'with the amount you give him to eat.'

'He sicks up most of it,' said Monica thoughtfully, in the voice of one who is on the brink of discovering the connection between effect and cause. Through a dense fringe of hair, Kiki stared up at her with infinite trust. And who am I to come between them, thought Edith.

'Anyway, he's not bad looking,' said Monica, lighting one of her immense cigarettes. 'Neville, I mean. And you're not bad looking, Edith, when you put your mind to it. Your clothes are terrible, if you don't mind my saying so. Or even if you do. Still, that's your affair. No, Mr Neville could be thought to be a catch.'

'I hadn't noticed,' said Edith truthfully.

Monica gave her a narrow glance. 'My dear girl, that man had a price on his head the minute he walked into the hotel.'

'Monica,' said Edith, startled. 'Do you mean you have fallen in love with Mr Neville?'

'Who said anything about love?' replied Monica, after a pause.

'Then what . . . ?'

'Oh, never mind, Edith. No, I'll pay for this. No, really, do let me. I'm going to, anyway.'

Edith, rubbing a patch of the steamy window clear, saw the grey mist advancing and felt herself begin to dissolve into it. This is when character tells, she thought. But her character, by which she had never set much store, seemed to have undergone a debilitating process recently, perhaps since the thoughts of last night, and she knew that the only remedy was work. I have done it before, she admonished herself, and I can do it again. Besides, I am getting behind with *Beneath the Visiting Moon*. I promised Harold I'd let him have it by Christmas. I haven't written anything for three days. No wonder I feel depressed. I need to get down to some work.

'I think I'll go back,' she said to Monica. 'I've got some letters to write. What will you do?'

'On a day like this, the only thing to do is to go to the hairdresser and have the works. The whole caboodle. Walk round that way with me. You're not in a hurry, are you?'

No, she was not in a hurry. And when the tall woman linked arms with her, she found herself touched and warmed by the contact, and, with the little dog bustling ahead through the leaves, they wandered slowly and silently along under the damp trees, aware of an impatient but genuine good will towards each other, just enough to sustain them against the onslaught of more painful memories that came to them unbidden and uncensored.

Women share their sadness, thought Edith. Their joy they like to show off to one another. Victory, triumph over the odds, calls for an audience. And that air of bustle and exigence sometimes affected by the sexually loquacious – that is for the benefit of other women. No solidarity then.

In the dead hour between two and three, when sensible people put their feet up or take a nap, Edith walked with

Monica under the lifeless trees by the lake shore. The day seemed interminable, yet neither was in a hurry to have done with it. It seemed to both of them in their separate ways that only the possession of this day held worse days at bay, that, for each of them, the seriousness of their respective predicaments had so far been material for satire or for ridicule or even for amusement. But that the characters who had furnished that satire or that amusement were now taking on a disturbing life of their own, were revealing capacities for command or caprice that threatened, although in a very obscure or oblique way, their own marginal existence. We both came here to get other people out of trouble, thought Edith; no one considered our hopes and wishes. Yet hopes and wishes are what should be proclaimed, most strenuously proclaimed, if anyone is to be jolted into the necessity of taking note of them, let alone the obligation to fulfil them. Yet how curious it is that some women have to be indulged and placated all the time ... It seems that I shall never learn the rules of correct behaviour, she thought, those rules that girls are supposed to learn at their mother's knee. All I learned I learned from Father. Think again, Edith. You have made a false equation. This is when character tells. Sad precepts of a lost faith.

With a sigh they turned round and began to walk back the way they had come, in the direction of the town and of the hairdresser. The streets were dull and empty, most people having prudently withdrawn from this unpromising scene. They rounded the corner and wandered past the bookshop; Edith, half-heartedly, hung back to look in the window, where *Le Soleil de Minuit*, in its paper cover, made a modest appearance. It was my best, she thought. But the prospect of doing it all over again, for the rest of my life, strikes a chill into my heart.

'Edith,' hissed Monica. 'Don't hurry.'

Mildly surprised, Edith looked up, and saw in the distance Mrs Pusey and Jennifer, arm in arm, emerging from a shop that sold gloves and handkerchiefs. An assistant, holding three of the shop's smartly decorated bags that were almost as hand-some as their contents, followed them after a moment or two and was directed to the car, which Edith and Monica could now perceive cruising slowly towards them from the opposite direction. The driver stopped, emerged from behind the wheel, crossed the street, conferred with the Puseys, took the parcels and got back into the car. Mrs Pusey, apparently restored to health and equilibrium by her purchases, could be seen smiling and nodding her head vigorously, although Monica and Edith were too far away to hear what was being said. Instinctively, they backed into the bookseller's doorway, in the hope of not being noticed. But after a minute or two it was clear that the attention of the Puseys was held in one of those intense and enthusiastic colloquies from which all outsiders were definitely disbarred. This realization, coming to them both simul-taneously, caused them to exchange a look in which relief and something like resignation were exactly mingled.

'The thing is,' said Monica, 'that we will either have to catch up with them or go past them or trail behind them in order to get back.'

'You were going to the hairdresser,' Edith reminded her.

'Well, that's on the way, isn't it? You'd have to come that far with me if you wanted to get back to the hotel.'

'I don't want to get back all that much,' said Edith, to whom the hotel or what it represented had become uncomfortable.

'In that case,' decided Monica, 'we might as well go back and have another coffee.'

They retraced their steps through the little stony grey street. By this time their earlier intimacy had fragmented into a sort of disaffection; each was inwardly sighing at the wasted day. I should have stayed in, thought Edith; I should have spent the day writing. At least when I am writing I am gainfully employed. This strolling about is pointless. Functionless. Yet it is only a day, and I have no real duties. and I am not letting anybody down. In a way it is quite pleasant, really, she thought, heavy-hearted, as they made their way once more into Haffenegger's, its interior now rich with the smell of sugar and coffee, and busy with the conversations of the immaculate, stolid, well-behaved ladies who made up the regular afternoon clientèle.

'Makes you homesick, doesn't it?' said Monica, who seemed quite reduced by the fact that the attention of the waitresses was now monopolized by those stern and hearty women who seemed to have displaced her. Her face registered the wistfulness she felt at being displaced, and she busied herself with installing Kiki on a spare chair, just in case anyone should come to claim it.

They sat islanded in their foreignness, irrelevant now that the holiday season had ended, anachronistic, outstaying their welcome, no longer necessary to anyone's plans. Priorities had shifted; the little town was settling down for its long uninterrupted hibernation. No one came here in the winter. The weather was too bleak, the snow too distant, the amenities too sparse to tempt visitors. And they felt that the backs of the residents had been turned on them with a sigh of relief, reminding them of their transitory nature, their fundamental unreality. And when Monica at last succeeded in ordering coffee, they still sat, glumly, for another ten minutes, before the busy waitress remembered their order.

'Homesick,' said Edith finally. 'Yes.' But she thought of her little house as if it had existed in another life, another dimension. She thought of it as something to which she might never return. The seasons had changed since she last saw it; she was no longer the person who could sit up in bed in the early morning and let the sun warm her shoulders and the light make her impatient for the day to begin. That sun, that light had faded, and she had faded with them. Now she was as grey as the season itself. She bent her head over her coffee, trying to believe that it was the steam rising from the cup that was making her eyes prick. This cannot go on, she thought.

'Oh, Christ,' moaned Monica. 'That does it. That's all we need.'

Edith, raising her head and following the direction of Monica's eyes, looked towards the doorway where Mrs Pusey, laughing, her arm through that of Mr Neville, was waiting for Jennifer to negotiate rights in a favourable table. The elderly man who had been sitting at the one she had chosen, and who had about to light a cigarette, changed his mind, gathered his briefcase and shopping bag from the empty seat beside him, and retired to the cash desk to pay his bill, while at the same time attempting to put on his hat and coat. As he left, he raised his hat to Jennifer, who beamed. She had, in that instant, Edith noted, exactly the same expression as her mother.

Monica and Edith sat hunched, furtive, waiting for the inevitable summons. This, however, was not forthcoming. Instead, after a few minutes, they found themselves watching the Puseys and Mr Neville. Much sparkling laughter was in evidence, at least from Mrs Pusey; an anecdote was being recounted by Jennifer, and Mr Neville, his head inclined indulgently in her direction, was paying grave attention. He was not saying anything, Edith noted. It was Mrs Pusey who was supplying the recitative.

'Well,' said Monica. 'I suppose we could make a move now.'

She seemed thoughtful. Edith sighed and called for the bill. They waited in silence for it to be delivered, then, cautiously, stood up and turned towards the door.

'Why,' said Mrs Pusey in surprise, as they edged past her table, 'there are the girls!' They stood awkwardly, smiling, as Jennifer and Mr Neville smiled back. 'And what have you two been doing with yourselves all day?' asked Mrs Pusey.

'Having a rest,' said Edith, rather uncertainly. 'Are you feeling better, Mrs Pusey?' She noted that Mrs Pusey's appearance, so refulgent from a distance, could be seen, at closer quarters, to be subject to a certain degree of disintegration. The cheekbones were rosier, the eyelids bluer, and the mouth

121

slightly more tremulous, more smudged, than usual. And yet the will was there, the indomitable will, the refusal to give up, give in, give way, stand down, stay behind. Admirable Mrs Pusey, thought Edith. Protected by the brilliance of her own *réclame*. She will outlive us all. But she repeated, 'Are you feeling better?'

Mrs Pusey cast her eyes down, then cast them up again.

'Yes, dear, thank you. Thanks to these two dear people, I'm almost myself again. Though when I think . . .'

'Must go,' said Monica. 'Hair appointment. Coming, Edith?' Edith mimed haste, regret, farewell into the upturned faces of the Puseys and Mr Neville, and followed Monica out into the street.

She scarcely remembered getting back to the hotel, although she shivered once more as the mist stole in from the lake. Back in her room, she ran a bath until the bathroom was dense with steam. She brushed her hair furiously and left it hanging loose on her shoulders. She studied her crimson face in the glass, then walked to the wardrobe and took out the new blue silk dress that Monica had made her buy and which she had never worn. She disappeared into the bathroom with a bottle of scent, and poured the entire contents into the water. Heat and rebellion and extravagance served her appearance well. An altogether different creature sat down at her writing table and uncapped her pen.

'My dearest David' (she wrote).

But caution warned her not to start her letter before dinner, because once started she could not be sure when she would stop.

She paced up and down in her room, unwilling to exchange her silence for the pleasantries of the evening. Eventually, with a sigh, she took up her bag and key and went downstairs.

In the salon, Mrs Pusey, in her black chiffon, was, as usual, accompanied by Jennifer, who looked pink and rested. The pianist, arranging his music, looked up enquiringly at Mrs Pusey who raised a deprecating hand and shook her head, as if to indicate that her attention was not available that evening. Discouraged, he began his usual selection, but without enthusiasm. Mme de Bonneuil came rocking in, paused, and went over to Mrs Pusey. '*Alors*,' she enquired, in her hoarse, loud, deaf voice. '*Ça va mieux, la santé?*' Mrs Pusey managed a tired smile, and waved a spotless handkerchief, but did not reply. Disconcerted, but only for a moment, because she was used to being ignored, Mme de Bonneuil turned away with a shrug. '*Toujours pomponnée*,' she observed, to herself, as she thought, but in fact to the assembled company. Mr Neville, elegant ankles crossed, remained in a far corner, obscured behind his newspaper. Edith, her head held high, advanced in his direction.

'Why, Edith,' cried Mrs Pusey, with her usual vivacity. 'What on earth have you done to your hair? Come and join us, dear. Let me have a proper look at you.'

Edith crept back to her accustomed seat, while Mrs Pusey, a finger to her chin, looked doubtful.

'Well, it's unusual, of course,' she pronounced finally. 'But I think I liked it better the other way. Jennifer! What do you think, darling?'

Jennifer, looking up from her nails, gave a brief vague smile. 'Quite nice,' she said. 'Not bad at all.'

'Oh, but I think I liked it better the other way,' said Mrs Pusey. And, with her head on one side, continued to assess the problem until it was time to go in to dinner.

11

Edith, stepping carefully and shivering a little in the chill air, took Mr Neville's outstretched hand. The landing stage was deserted; the prospect was too poor to tempt visitors, such as the few that were left, to a day trip on the lake. It was in fact the last such trip of the season, a fact held out by Mr Neville as an inducement. He seemed to collect such uncomfortable and out of the way experiences, expecting from them nothing but the value of novelty and irony. For this brief excursion he was, once again, hopelessly well dressed. Two American ladies, wearing trousers and plastic mackintoshes, contemplated his greenish tweed suit and his deerstalker hat from behind the glass of the verandah-like cabin. There was no one on the deck. To Edith, it seemed as if there were no one else on the ship which slid, very silently, away from the shore and into the grey mist that encompassed the lake as far as the eye could see.

Mr Neville took up an elegant position, his hands on the rail. Edith, shuddering in time with the steady throb of the engine, turned her back on the desolate scene, trying to limit her vision to the structure which supported her, but a feeling of being cut off, not only from dry land, but from any recognizable viewpoint, unsteadied her. Out of sheer weakness she had left herself no means of escape, a fact of which she was uncomfortably aware. I could have stayed in and spent the entire day writing, she thought to herself, but the mere thought of it made me feel ill. The fact is that there are very few distractions in a place like this and one gets to fear one's own boredom. It is not true that Satan makes work for idle hands to do; that is just what he doesn't. Satan should be at hand with all manner of glittering distractions, false but irresistible promises, inducements to reprehensible behaviour. Instead of which one is simply offered a choice between overwork and half-hearted idleness. And that is scarcely a choice at all. One cannot even rely on Satan to fulfil his obligations.

'Now what?' asked Mr Neville, taking her arm.

'Oh, nothing,' said Edith. 'I was simply thinking how little vice there is around these days. One is led to believe that one can pick and choose, but in fact there seems to be no choice at all.'

'Stroll round the deck with me,' said Mr Neville. 'You are shivering. That cardigan is not warm enough; I do wish you would get rid of it. Whoever told you that you looked like Virginia Woolf did you a grave disservice, although I suppose you thought it was a compliment. As to vice, there is plenty to be found if you know where to look.'

'I never seem to find it,' said Edith.

'That is because you do not give yourself over wholeheartedly to the pursuit. But, if you remember, we are going to change all that.'

'I really don't see how. If all it involves is giving away my cardigan, I feel I should tell you that I have another one at home. Of course, I could give that away too. But I seem to be too spiritless for radical improvement. I am simply not fascinating. I don't know why.'

'No,' he said. 'One sees that.'

He pulled her hand more firmly through his arm and steered her forward. 'Round once more,' he instructed her. 'You are getting your colour back. The air will do you nothing but good. Fair-skinned women should be out as much as possible. They cannot afford to languish indoors; their faces disappear altogether. Brace yourself, Edith. When you feel a little warmer you will begin to relax and enjoy yourself. That's better. But there is no need to look so grim. This is, after all, a pleasure steamer.'

Edith gazed at the measureless grey expanse of the lake. The steamer was unhurried, silent; now that her ears had got used to the very slight vibration of the engine she could pick up other sounds: the tiny suction of the waves on the side, far below, the creaking of the wings of a gull-like bird which flew low over the deck, the flapping of her thin skirt as it blew

125

against her legs. And yet there was no wind, nothing but a steady pressure forward, without any discernible progress being made. Somewhere behind the veils of mist there was a pale sun which could be seen, in the far distance, to cast a white gleam on the water. They were to land at Ouchy, where they would lunch, and to come back in the afternoon. But it seemed to Edith that this journey was too serious to be thought of simply in terms of diversion. The empty lake, the fitful light, the dream-like slowness with which they were covering the distance, seemed to have an allegorical significance. Ships, she knew, were often used by painters as symbols of the soul, sometimes of the soul departing for unknown shores. Of death, in fact. Or, if not of death, not of anything very hopeful. Ship of fools, slave ship, shipwreck, storm at sea: such representations, even if not expert, working on that fear that lies dormant even in the strongest heart, upset the nerves and the balance, for such was their intention. Edith, once again, felt unsafe, distressed, unhoused.

She rather wished that she had not accepted his invitation, but, coming as it did after her fruitless day with Monica, it had seemed attractive. There was, moreover, a considerable force of will hidden behind Mr Neville's correctly tailored persona, and Edith had found it difficult to dissuade him from his original purpose. This banal and inappropriate excursion seemed to her almost perverse in its lack of attractions; she had supposed that they might be going on another walk, a ruminative mode that suited her even when laced with the sort of anarchic suggestion for which Mr Neville had, in her eyes, become mildly precious. But no, he had forced her on to this terrible boat, this almost deserted and pilotless vessel, from which there was no hope of rescue; she saw them drifting, their aimlessness raised to almost mythological status, into ever thicker mists, while real people, on the shore, went on with their real lives, indifferent to this ghost ship which seemed, to Edith, almost to have passed out of normal existence. For this reason she clung rather tightly to Mr Neville's arm, for, although himself a curiously mythological personage, he never-theless managed to represent a most tangible reality.

Yet slowly, and perhaps because Mr Neville obligingly remained silent, her nerves yielded to the prevailing mournful calm, and as the landing stage at Ouchy began to materialize, she was able to take a deep breath and to relax her tight hold on Mr Neville's impeccable greenish sleeve.

'There,' he said, as they stepped out into a lakeside restaurant surrounded by potted hydrangeas. 'That wasn't too bad, was it?'

'I am actually quite glad to be surrounded by all these waiters and bottles and millionaires,' Edith confessed. 'At least I assume they are millionaires?'

'That is what they would like you to assume, certainly. And if money talks, as it is supposed to, then they are certainly making the right amount of noise.'

He settled her at a table in the shade of a striped awning, picked up the menu which an attentive waiter had immediately placed before him, and said, 'I should have the duck if I were you.'

Edith ignored him. 'I lost my bearings out there, I think. I felt as if we might not be allowed back.'

'Is there so much to go back to?' enquired Mr Neville. 'No,' he said. 'I'm sorry. Perhaps that was impertinent. Please forgive me. You may not be fascinating, Edith, but you certainly know how to make a man feel uncomfortable.'

Edith smiled demurely. 'Am I to take that as a compliment?' she asked.

Mr Neville rewarded her with a cold look. 'That is the sort of remark I associate with a lesser woman. You are unsettling. Simply leave it at that. You don't have to dimple and bridle, like an ingénue. Am I to take that as a compliment, indeed. I hope you are not going to turn into the kind of woman who leans across the table, props her chin in her hand, and says, "What are you thinking?"'

'All right, all right,' said Edith, with a sudden return of

joviality. 'I am not here to pass tests, you know. I am supposed to be enjoying myself.'

'You will find that the one does not preclude the other,' said Mr Neville, his ambiguous smile hovering around his mouth. But he ordered a fine lunch, and as the duck was placed before her, he was glad to see her expression brighten and her colour return. His own duck despatched by means of a few expertly calculated incisions, he leaned back to light a cigar. A weak sun emerged. Edith sat still and lifted her face, idle now, and in no hurry.

'Talking of going back,' said Mr Neville, 'what did you have in mind? I do not mean back to the hotel; that is inevitable. I mean back to your ordinary life. I only ask,' he added, 'because I myself must leave at the weekend.'

Edith's smile faded. The thought of going home, or rather, back, would have to be faced, but she found herself unwilling to contemplate taking so decisive an action. This curious interlude in her life, uncomfortable though it was, had relieved her of the necessity of thinking about what was to come. And this moment, becalmed on this stone-floored platform, at this agreeable open-air restaurant, with a companion of really unusual character and perception, had had the further result of enabling her successfully to postpone any deeper thoughts.

Tilted back in his chair, Mr Neville watched her face. 'Let me see,' he said mildly. 'Let me see if I can imagine what your life is like. You live in London. You have a comfortable income. You go to drinks parties and dinner parties and publishers' parties. You do not really enjoy any of this. Although people are glad to see you, you lack companions of first resort. You come home alone. You are fussy about your house. You have had lovers but not half as many as your friends have had; they, of course, credit you with none at all and worry about you rather ostentatiously. You are aware of this. And yet you have a secret life, Edith. Although only too obviously incorruptible, you are not what you seem.'

Edith sat very still.

Mr Neville deposited the ash of his cigar carefully in the ashtray.

'Of course, you will say that this is none of my business. I would say, simply, that it does not concern me. Any more than my diversions need concern you. Whatever arrangements we may come to must leave these considerations scrupulously unexamined.'

'Arrangements?' echoed Edith.

Mr Neville sat forward and put his hands on the table. He seemed, suddenly, somewhat younger and less controlled than usual. It had been easy to think of him as a wealthy man in his fifties, fastidious, careful, leisured, attractive in a bloodless sort of way, the kind of man who gave great thought to his way of life, a man in whom appetite might turn to some anodyne hobby, the collecting of drypoint etchings or the tracing of his own family tree. The kind of man who would undoubtedly have a fine library but whom it was somehow difficult to imagine in any other room of a house.

'I think you should marry me, Edith,' he said.

She stared at him, her eyes widening in disbelief.

'Let me explain,' he said, rather hurriedly, taking a firm grip on his composure. 'I am not a romantic youth. I am in fact extremely discriminating. I have a small estate and a very fine house, Regency Gothic, a really beautiful example. And I have a rather well-known collection of *famille rose* dishes. I am sure you love beautiful things.'

'You are wrong,' she said, her voice cold. 'I do not love *things* at all.'

'I have a lot of business overseas,' he went on, ignoring her. 'And I like to entertain. I am away a certain amount of the time. But I dislike having to come back to a house only occupied by the couple who live in it when I am not there. You would fit perfectly into that setting.'

A terrible silence installed itself between them. Edith concentrated her attention on the bill, fluttering unnoticed under an ashtray. When she spoke her voice was unsteady.

129

'You make it sound like a job specification,' she said. 'And I have not applied for the job.'

'Edith, what else will you do? Will you too go back to an empty house?'

She shook her head, wordless.

'You see,' he went on, 'I cannot afford another scandal. My wife's adventure made me look a laughing stock. I thought I could sit it out with dignity, but dignity doesn't help. Rather the opposite. People seem to want you to break down. However, that's all in the past. I need a wife, and I need a wife whom I can trust. It has not been easy for me.'

'And you are not making it easy for me,' she said.

'I am making it easier for you. I have watched you, trying to talk to those women. You are desolate. And without the sort of self-love which I have been urging on you, you are never going to learn the rules, or you are going to learn them too late and become bitter. And when you think you are alone, your expression is full of sorrow. You face a life of exile of one sort or another.'

'But why should you think me such a hopeless case?'

'You are a lady, Edith. They are rather out of fashion these days, as you may have noticed. As my wife, you will do very well. Unmarried, I'm afraid you will soon look a bit of a fool.'

She studied him sadly. 'And what will I do in your fine house, when you are away?' she asked. And when you are not away, she thought, but kept the thought to herself.

'Whatever you do now, only better. You may write, if you want to. In fact, you may begin to write rather better than you ever thought you could. Edith Neville is a fine name for an author. You will have a social position, which you need. You will gain confidence, sophistication. And you will have the satisfaction of knowing that you are doing me credit. You are not the sort of woman of whom men are afraid, hysterics who behave as though they are the constant object of scandal or desire, who boast of their conquests and their performance, and who think they can do anything so long as they entertain their friends and keep a minimal bargain with their husbands.'

'Women too are afraid of that sort of woman,' murmured Edith.

'No,' he said. 'Most women *are* that sort of woman.'

She looked up at him. 'But I thought that men preferred that kind of woman. I thought that they despised the sort of conjugal peace that you prescribe for me.'

'In a sense, yes,' he replied. 'Men do like that kind of woman. They feel they are missing out if they get anything that is less than tricky and fantastic; they like the danger of that sort of attachment. They like the feeling that they have had to fight other men for possession. That is what it is all about, really. Knocking other men down. It is only when those other men get up and start fighting for possession all over again that they realize how fragile, how *tiring*, that particular kind of partnership is. One gets no work done.'

'Again you are paying me the tremendous compliment of assuming that no one else will want me, ever.'

'I am paying you the compliment of assuming that you know the difference between flirtation and fidelity. I am paying you the compliment of assuming that you will never indulge in the sort of gossipy indiscretions that so discredit a man. I am paying you the compliment of believing that you will not shame me, will not ridicule me, *will not hurt my feelings*. Do you realize how hard it is for a man to own up to being hurt in that way? I simply cannot afford to let it happen again.'

'And yet the other day you were preaching a doctrine of selfishness. Centrality was your word. How is that to be shared?'

'Much more easily than you think. I am not asking you to lose all for love. I am asking you to recognize your own true self-interest. I am simply telling you what you may already have begun to suspect: that modesty and merit are very poor cards to hold. I am proposing a partnership of the most enlightened kind. A partnership based on esteem, if you like. Also out of fashion, by the way. If you wish to take a lover, that is your concern, so long as you arrange it in a civilized manner.'

'And if you . . .'

'The same applies, of course. For me, now, that would always be a trivial matter. You would not hear of it nor need you care about it. The union between us would be one of shared interests, of truthful discourse. Of companionship. To me, now, these are the important things. And for you they should be important. Think, Edith. Have you not, at some time in your well-behaved life, desired vindication? Are you not tired of being polite to rude people?'

Edith bowed her head.

'You will be able to entertain your friends, of course. And you will find that they treat you quite differently. This comes back to what I was saying before. You will find that you can behave as badly as you like. As badly as everybody else likes, too. That is the way of the world. And you will be respected for it. People will at last feel comfortable with you. You are lonely, Edith.'

After a long pause she looked up and said, 'It's getting cold. Shall we go back?'

The lake steamer had taken on board a party of school-children, very young, some of whose heads only reached to just above the guard rail. They were not given to excess or noise, and once the ship had left the shore they were summoned into the glassed-off observation lounge by their teacher for some sort of lesson. Obediently, they turned like swallows and left Edith and Mr Neville alone on deck.

It was colder now and the afternoon was fading. A little wind had blown up, forerunner of colder winds to come, bringing with it the thought of winter. Edith seemed to see her house, shut up, no fires lit, dust settling, letters unopened on the mat, the windows dirty, the rooms airless, neglected, old smells of food clinging to the curtains. And herself forgotten, the telephone not ringing. Crossed off the lists of invitations to publishers' parties by brisk young secretaries impatient at not getting any response. Her agent, kind Harold, writing her off with a shake of the head. And of David, what news? If she went back, could she bear to find out how he felt, whether he would welcome her return? And if he were not there? Where would she find him? Anything might have happened to him in her absence; perhaps he was on holiday, was ill, was dead. Or perhaps he was quite happy with things as they were. The wind tore at her hair and with a gesture of anguish she pulled it loose from its pins and let it stream across her face. Is it true? she thought. Was I the sort of placid faithful woman who could not keep his interest? Was I simply unusual and discreet, the sort who can be relied upon not to make a fuss, such a rest from his tricky and fantastic and provocative wife? Was I simply a rather touching interlude for him, or did he think me far more practised than I was? Did he assume that I was doing the same thing, with the same degree of selfishness, as he was?

'Edith,' said Mr Neville. 'Please don't cry. I cannot bear to see a woman cry; it makes me want to hit her. Please, Edith. Here, take my handkerchief. Edith. Let me wipe your eyes. Your eyes are almost silver. Did you know that? Come.'

For the first time she rested against him and cried herself into a state of weariness. She closed her eyes and stayed leaning on his shoulder, steadied by his arm.

'You are very thin,' he said. 'I am afraid that I might break you in half. But there will be time to worry about that later.'

When she straightened up and stood with her hands on the rail, she saw that it was already dusk, or rather an afternoon twilight that would deepen imperceptibly into night. On the opposite shore she could make out lights, lights that seemed almost welcoming now: the lights of the Hotel du Lac.

They leaned against the rail, not speaking. When the landing stage came into view, he turned to her, but she held up her hand for him to be silent. The children, once more marshalled on the deck by their teacher, must be untouched by the miasma of these adult considerations. As they trooped off, their shoes pattering on the wooden boards, Edith and

133

Mr Neville remained standing silently at the rail, facing the shore.

'So', she said, after a long silence. 'I am to live in your house – Regency Gothic; a fine example – along with your *famille rose* dishes. I am to be air-lifted out of my present life, as if a wand had been waved. I am to become sophisticated, relaxed, worldly, and discreet. I am to provide that conjugal calm that will ensure that your feelings will never be hurt again.'

'And yours,' he said. 'And yours.'

'I don't love you. Does that bother you?'

'No. It reassures me. I do not want the burden of your feelings. All this can be managed without romantic expectations.'

Edith turned to him. Her hair blew in eddies round her head, her eyes were grave, her mouth bitter.

'And you don't love me?'

He smiled, this time sadly and without ambiguity.

'No, I don't love you. But you have got under my guard. You have moved and touched me, in a way in which I no longer care to be moved and touched. You are like a nerve that I had managed to deaden, and I am annoyed to find it coming to life. I shall do my utmost to kill it off again as soon as possible. After all, I am not in the business of losing *my* centrality. We must get off, Edith. Give me your hand.'

They walked in silence, hand in hand, over the soft wooden boards of the landing stage and on to the gravel path. Now the mist was coming down again, with the dusk, blurring the street lamps, veiling the everyday sounds. The modest evening traffic was almost over, and a chill spread from the untenanted lake behind them.

'I may have to think about this,' she said eventually.

'Not too long, I hope. I do not intend to make a habit of proposing to you. You will have to get your skates on, if we are to leave by the weekend.'

She glanced up at him, surprised by the new jocularity in his voice. It seemed to her that he had already effected such repairs to his self-esteem as he deemed necessary, and she was a little encouraged by the rapidity with which this had been achieved.

'May I ask one more question?' she said.

'Of course.'

'Why me?'

This time his smile was ambiguous again, ironic, courteous.

'Perhaps because you are harder to catch than the others,' he replied.

12

Bathed and changed, her hair once more firmly secured, Edith sat in her room, waiting for it to be time to go down to dinner.

It seemed to her then that she had finished with this room, or perhaps that the room had finished with her. In any event, some sort of natural conclusion had been reached. Yet, just as it is in the nature of leavetaking to feel regret, she knew that this room, in which she had been entirely alone, would always awaken in her some memory of warmth whenever she summoned it to mind. Its silent, faded dignity would perhaps come to symbolize the last shred of her own dignity, before that too crumbled in the face of panic, or bravado, or just cold common sense.

It was the very coldness of her common sense that was afflicting her with this almost senile tremor. Abruptly she got up and went to the window; drawing aside the curtain she could see nothing but blackness, and the only sound she could hear was the occasional swish of tyres. For the weather had broken, and the mist had dissolved into a mournful drizzle; the clinging damp had the slow persistence of a climate that has at last found its natural mode of expression. So she would not be able to sit out on her balcony, writing at the green tin table, as she had intended. But in any event the book had not taken off, was destined, perhaps from the start, to be abandoned. And yet I have always, as an act of will, written myself back into a state of acceptance, she thought. Why does the recipe no longer work? Is it because the whole process now seems too much like the hair shirt of the penitent, angling to get back into God's good graces? Am I just sick to death of making yet another effort? Will it not be very comfortable not to have to make this particular effort any more? And she passed a vale-dictory hand over her precisely written sheets of manuscript before putting them back in their folder, and putting the folder into the bottom of her travel bag.

This action startled her, as if her plans had been made final without her having reached any conscious decision. Yet the fact that she had accepted them as final was demonstrated by the way in which she started to fold and pack the dresses she would no longer wear here, and, as the process gathered momentum, her almost precipitous bundling together of shoes, books, scent bottles, until all that remained of her life at the Hotel du Lac was her nightgown, her hairbrush, and the clothes she was wearing. Then, having nothing more to do in this room, which was once more impersonal, ready to receive the next guest at the beginning of the new season, she closed the door behind her and made her way down the stairs to the salon.

Here too the absence of activity seemed to signify a general decision to leave. The pianist had worked out his engagement and would now return to his winter occupation of giving private lessons to unmusical schoolgirls. M. Huber, slightly disappointed, as always, at having somehow failed to achieve that ideal and brilliant social mix which is the hotelier's most persistent wish, viewed the empty salon with regret. He was feeling those rheumatic twinges that heralded both the winter and his exile, for he was to proceed, once the Hotel du Lac shut down, to the Spanish villa of his daughter and son-in-law, where he languished in the eventless sunshine, with nothing to supervise: he was no good at being a guest. In another week they would close down. Mme de Bonneuil would be transported, by her son, to her stoically endured winter quarters, a religious *pension* in Lausanne. The woman with the dog would go home, a prospect which had already brought a flush of agitation and excitement to her handsome face. Mme Pusey and her daughter, for whom he felt the most affection, would be chauffeur-driven to Geneva, where they would catch a plane and pay a very great deal of money for excess baggage, but he liked to think of them passing directly from his care to the safety of their London apartment. A charming woman, charming; the daughter perhaps a little less distinguished.

137

Cards would be exchanged in due course, for they kept in touch. And they would no doubt meet here again the following year, if they were spared. The other two remaining guests were of little interest to him; they were too recent, and he knew that they would not be back.

The staff, released from the tight restraints of their normal good behaviour, made more noise among themselves, talked to each other quite openly. Alain and Maryvonne, who turned out to be cousins, would be going back to Fribourg, and would spend the winter working in Maryvonne's father's restaurant. The manager, as usual, made fruitless plans to persuade his father-in-law to retire for good, while at the same time facing up to the fact that this would never happen.

For a while Edith sat alone in the salon, remembering her first evening here. Too much had happened to make this process entirely comfortable. Looking back, she saw that on that occasion she had been braver, younger, more determined to sit out her banishment and to return home unchanged by it. It had seemed, at the time, almost a joke, or perhaps she had simply decided to see it in that light. Since then she felt as if she had acquired an adult's seriousness for the first time in her life and that henceforth all decisions would have that prudent weightiness that she had never thought hers to exercise by right. She was about to enter a world which she had instinctively recognized as belonging to others, in which she had no claim, a world of, among other things, investments, roof repairs, visitors for the weekend. And shall we take your car or mine? That was one of the remarks that she had overheard David make to his wife, and it had come to possess an almost totemic significance. Behind it she had glimpsed a series of assumptions with which they had both, equally, grown up. Launched young into adult enjoyment, fearless, privileged, spoilt, they retained a similar impatience with anything serious or disheartening, were quick, charming, enthusiastic, and forgetful. Depths were not easily reached with them and their kind. But Edith, who had spent the years of her youth in silence and wariness, and who, in order to outwit disappointment, had learnt not to make claims, was acquainted with those depths, and was, at this solemn moment, lost in contemplation before she left them for ever.

When she raised her eyes she saw that the dark shadow by the far pillar had resolved itself into the shape of Mme de Bonneuil, who had presumably been there all the time. Hands clasped on her stick, her dusty veil shedding its last sequins on to the shoulders of her equally dusty black dress, Mme de Bonneuil too seemed to be contemplating her imminent removal. But for Mme de Bonneuil, thought Edith with a pang, it would not be removal to a world of enviable adult preoccupations. She imagined a dark little room in Lausanne, and less food, less service, less dignity. And what would she do all day? The absurd terrain of Lausanne would be too difficult for her to negotiate, even with a stick. And the winter would be long, very long. As the waiters appeared in the doorways of the salon, Edith got up, went over to Mme de Bonneuil, and offered her an arm. A pleased but puzzled smile flickered doubtfully across the latter's face, but at that moment Monica, skittish and beautiful in a flame-coloured dress, her life and energy restored by the prospect of going home, strolled out of the bar and called, 'Wait for me!' Mme de Bonneuil, each arm securely tethered, her stick carried by Alain, proceeded, accompanied by Edith and Monica, into the dining room, her head held high, her expression worldly, her demeanour superior to her surroundings. As M. Huber hastened forward to greet her ('And about time too,' said Monica scornfully), Mme de Bonneuil pressed both the younger women's hands warmly before acknowledging him with a minimal nod. Her chair adjusted by a solicitous waiter, Mme de Bonneuil turned her attention calmly to the menu, but throughout dinner her head remained high and from time to time her smile returned.

Dinner was half-way through before Mrs Pusey, in fine lilac wool, made her entrance. Once again Edith marvelled at her appearance. Her full figure, her shining blonde hair, her cloud of scent almost obscured the presence of Jennifer who, although equally well accoutred, signalled something cruder, less exquisite, less highly conscious, less ardently attached to these repeated pleasantries. As M. Huber rose, predictably, from his seat to welcome Mrs Pusey and to guide her to her table, Edith, watching as always with fascinated interest, found her attention drawn to the enigmatic Jennifer, who, indifferent to the chill of the evening, was wearing another of her oddly immodest outfits, a clinging low-necked blue silk sweater and a pair of white knickerbockers. Yet although her appearance was that of a large rich teenager about to be taken off in some-body's car for an evening at a smart discothèque, she was as assiduous as ever in her attentions to her mother whose conversation was apparently all that she required by way of social stimulus. Edith continued to watch as the napkins were flourished, the wine poured, the bread broken, the soup savoured with much closing of the eyes in delicate appreci-ation; they were apparently unaware, Edith noted, that there was anyone else in the room but themselves or that the meal had been prepared for any other purpose than to assuage their own unassailable appetites.

Taking coffee in the salon, Edith found herself treated a little distantly by Mrs Pusey. Perhaps her return earlier that evening with Mr Neville had been noted, and filed away without comment. In any event, Edith was obliged to listen to Mrs Pusey's plans, which were, as usual, extensive, without being awarded any interest in her own. Reciprocity was a state unknown to Mrs Pusey, whose imperative need for social dominance, once assured by her beauty and the mute presence of an adoring husband, had now to be enforced by more brutal means. Not that there was anything brutal in her charming recital of the labours of packing that awaited them – the very thought gave her a headache – and the arrangements that had yet to be made with her housekeeper, who would dispatch a car to meet them at Heathrow, and who would have a light supper ready on trays for Mrs Pusey and Jennifer to eat in Mrs Pusey's bedroom.

'I'm a wreck after travelling,' confided Mrs Pusey to Edith.

'Yet you've done so much,' Edith replied.

'Yes, well, I owed it to my husband. He wouldn't go anywhere without me. Said he couldn't bear to be away from me, the silly man.'

She laughed reminiscently. 'And it becomes a habit, you know. Of course, I couldn't do it without Jennifer. And she's still willing to put up with her old mother, aren't you, darling?'

Again the loving clasp of hands, the kiss, the radiant smiles. Yet Edith had seen Jennifer looking, for her, almost thoughtful, her normally indifferent expression less well-intentioned than usual. But with the loving exchange this was wiped away. I must have imagined it, thought Edith. I am morbid this evening.

'When will you leave?' she asked.

'Oh, we'll stay until the end of next week, if they'll put up with us.' Again, a little laugh.

'I . . .' she began, but was interrupted by Mrs Pusey's cry, 'Why, there's Philip! Where have you been, you naughty man? Jennifer thought you'd abandoned us. Darling, get Philip some fresh coffee. Why were you so late?'

'I had some calls to make,' he said, surrendering to her demands with every appearance of alacrity. 'And the lines seemed to be permanently engaged.'

'Business calls, I suppose,' said Mrs Pusey, with an understanding tilt of her head. 'I know. My husband always had to make his calls, wherever we were. I used to threaten to have the telephone removed sometimes. "Never mix business with pleasure," I used to say to him. Not that he ever let business come first, not when he had me with him, anyway.'

'Certain arrangements always have to be made,' said Mr Neville with a smile.

'Arrangements? That sounds as if you're going to leave us. Jennifer! Philip's going to leave us on our own.'

141

Jennifer looked up from her nails and gave a brief smile.

'I shall be leaving the day after tomorrow,' said Mr Neville in a neutral voice.

'Then we must make the most of you while we can,' cried Mrs Pusey. 'I hope you don't intend to disappear again tomorrow. We waited ages for you this morning, didn't we, darling?'

Clearly, thought Edith, I am to be invisible until I agree to his terms. And he is right. This is what it is like, and what it will always be like, if I don't marry him. This is what he is letting me see. Very well. But first there is something I must do.

In the silence that ensued, she recognized that the moment of decision had arrived.

She stood up. 'If you will excuse me . . .' she began.

'Yes, of course, Edith. Good night, dear.'

'Please don't get up,' said Edith to Mr Neville, placing a hand rather firmly on his shoulder. She did not care if this was construed as familiarity. She was suddenly very tired of being reticent. He could have said something, she thought, acutely aware of the pregnant silence behind her retreating back. And Mrs Pusey will spend the rest of the evening trying to find out what he will good-humouredly refuse to tell her. I am not needed.

Although her steps were light and silent, it seemed to her that she was trudging up the stairs like a weary traveller. And in the dim pinkish room, so serious, so quiet, she sat down once more like an exile. Finally, she moved over to the little table, took a sheet of paper, and wrote.

'My dearest David,

'This is the last letter that I shall ever write to you and the first one that I shall ever post. I am going to marry Philip Neville, a man I met here; I am going to live in his house near Marlborough, and I do not think that I shall ever see you again.

'You are the breath of life to me. One should not say such things, I know. You do not want to hear them. When I spoke those words to Penelope she looked aghast, affronted, as if I had dealt myself out of normal society by confessing as much. And so it seems that I have burnt too many boats, crossed too many bridges, ever to return to what I was before, or what I thought I was.

'I do not love Mr Neville, nor does he love me. But he has made me see what I will become if I persist in loving you as I do. I had begun to see this before I came here, and perhaps that wretched business with poor Geoffrey was the result of what I had begun to see. That fiasco will be avoided this time, mainly because Mr Neville will see that it is. He assures me that I will very soon, under his guidance, develop into the sort of acceptable woman whose confidence and stamina and indeed presumption I have always envied. Rather like your wife, in fact.

'I have never been a great success in this way, and so it was supremely ironical that I should fall in love with a man who has always been a success in every way. I lived for you. Yet how often did I see you? Perhaps twice a month? More, if we met by accident. Sometimes less, if you were too busy. And sometimes a whole month without you. I have imagined you at home, with your wife, and your children, and those times were bad. But much worse were the times when I suspected that your attention, your curiosity, had been aroused by somebody new, some girl whom you might have met somewhere, at a party, perhaps, as you once met me. And then I would scrutinize women in the street, in the bus, in the shops, looking for a face that I could fit into your fantasy. Because, you see, although I lack the details, I know you very well.

'I know, you see, that whatever you feel for me, or perhaps I should say, once felt for me, I am, as Swann said of Odette, not your type.

'There is no reason why we should ever meet again, except, of course, by accident. Mr Neville, who has a fine collection of *famille rose* dishes, no doubt spends a certain amount of time in the salerooms and auction houses, and it is just conceivable that he may wish me to accompany him on these visits. But I have told him of my indifference to collecting and I doubt if he will insist.

'I shall try to be a good wife to him. One does not receive proposals of marriage every day in this enlightened age, although curiously enough I have had two this year. I seem to have accepted them both. The lure of domestic peace was obviously too great for one of my timorous nature to resist. But I shall settle down now. I shall have to, for I doubt if I have anything more to look forward to.

'You thought, perhaps, like my publisher, and my agent, who are always trying to get me to bring my books up to date and make them sexier and more exciting, that I wrote my stories with that mixture of satire and cynical detachment that is thought to become the modern writer in this field. You were wrong. I believed every word I wrote. And I still do, even though I realize now that none of it can ever come true for me.

'You have known my address for the past two weeks, but I have not heard from you. There is therefore no point in telling you where I shall be living, for I shall not hear from you there either.

'I do not know how to end this letter. I do not want to succumb to reproaches, recriminations, and indeed I have no right to any of these things. To say that I was a willing partner is risible, for I was the more willing of the two. I was more willing than you.

'I send you all my love, always.

                                              Edith.'

She sat with her head in her hands for a long time, in the room now totally silent. She was not aware of time passing. Instead she seemed to look back into the past, to other times when silence had been her lot. When she had stood at the window of her house, listening to the vanishing hum of David's car. When, wordless, she had watched her father tidy his desk for the last time, or had meekly taken her mother's spilt coffee back to the kitchen. Even further back, she saw herself hiding behind Grossmama Edith's chair in the grim apartment in Vienna, while her mother and her aunts aired their grievances. And if she heard any words, they were quite inappropriate to her present situation. '*Schrecklich! Schrecklich!*' she heard Tante Resi shout. '*Ach, du Schreck!*'

When she got up, it occurred to her that she should go to bed, but her most imperative desire was not for sleep but for the morning, when she would take her letter to the post and thus ensure that there should be no second thoughts. She looked at her watch and saw that it was half-past one. She undressed and lay down on her bed, determined to last out the night and not weaken. Her cheeks burned, and she trembled slightly, but as the night deepened, her muscles relaxed, and her breathing slowed, and finally she slept.

When she awoke it was still dark, but she got up and bathed her face and hands; there would be time for a bath later, when she came back. She re-read her letter, put it in an envelope, and stuck it down. She dressed and brushed her hair. She was now quite calm, and sat patiently until she knew that there would be someone at the desk who could sell her a stamp. At six o'clock, unable to wait any longer, she picked up her bag and her key, opened her door very quietly, and stepped out into the corridor.

Making her way silently along the thick carpet, anxious not to awaken or alarm the sleeping guests, she was just in time to see Jennifer's door open and Mr Neville, in his dressing gown, emerge. With a caution equal to her own, he concentrated on making no noise, and pulled the door to very slowly. In the dim light left burning overnight she could quite clearly make out his controlled and ambiguous smile.

Of course, she thought. Of course.

She waited, frozen, until Mr Neville, unaware of her presence, turned away, walked rapidly along the corridor, and disappeared from sight.

And back in her room she realized how little surprised she was. She remembered his talk of preserving his centrality, repairing his self-esteem, noble words which she had perhaps accepted too easily. But that was not it, not entirely it. And then she remembered. When she had leaned against him and wept, and when he had put his arm around her, she had been aware that he had felt nothing. That he had returned her to herself most gracefully, but had felt nothing.

And Jennifer was no doubt one of those trivial diversions of which he spoke so dismissively. And that door, opening and shutting, in her dreams, in her delusive waking moments, had been a real door, the reality and implications of which she had failed to take into account.

She saw her father's patient face. Think again, Edith. You have made a false equation.

She sat down slowly on the bed, feeling a little faint. And if I were to marry him, she said to herself, knowing this, knowing too that he could so easily and so quickly look elsewhere, I should turn to stone, to paste: I should become part of his collection. But perhaps that is what he intended, she thought; that I should replace the item that was missing. And for me, those pleasures which are lightly called physical would remain where they have been for so long now, so long for me that they have become my lifetime. And I should lose the only life that I have ever wanted, even though it was never mine to call my own. And Mr Neville's smile, so unfailingly ambiguous, would always remind me of this.

After a while she got up.

Crossing over to the table, she picked up her letter, tore it in half, and dropped the pieces into the waste-paper basket. Then she took her bag and her key and left the room, went along the corridor and down the stairs. In the still silent hotel, the night porter waiting to go off duty, yawned behind the desk and scratched his head. He straightened up when he saw Edith, and hastily assumed a morning smile.

'I should like you to get me a ticket on the next flight to London,' she said, in a clear voice. 'And I should like to send a telegram.'

When the requisite form had been found, she sat down at a small glass table in the lobby. 'Simmonds, Chiltern Street, London W1,' she wrote. 'Coming home.' But, after a moment, she thought that this was not entirely accurate and, crossing out the words 'Coming home,' wrote simply, 'Returning.'

Notes to help you with your reading

The notes in this edition are intended to serve the needs of overseas students as well as those of British-born users.

Chapter 1

1 *spreading like an anaesthetic:* literally like a drug which puts you to sleep. The suggestion is that the lake is huge, dark, and all-enveloping.

   sparkling with emblematic significance: as though it were symbolic or representative of something.

   as if an access of good will could pierce the mysterious opacity with which she had been presented: ... as if the fog could be cleared by an effort of optimism and good will. The fog, of course, is not only the dense cloud covering the lake, but the strange uncertainty that seems to fill Edith's mind.

2 *inimical:* hostile.

3 *'Beneath the Visiting Moon':* the title of a romantic novel Edith is writing. The words are a quotation from Shakespeare's *Antony and Cleopatra*, spoken by Cleopatra to show her passionate feelings for Antony after he has killed himself. Once he is dead she feels that

   There is nothing left remarkable
       Beneath the visiting moon.

                                        (Act 4, scene 8, line 64)

   Such a title gives emphasis to the romantic content of the novel.

   hiatus: gap, breaking off before starting again.

   A cold coming I had of it: this is a reference to the first line

of 'The Journey of the Magi' by T. S. Eliot. The Wise
Men travelled through very difficult conditions to reach
Bethlehem. Edith Hope uses it to emphasise the coldness
of Penelope's responses to her. It is also an example of
Edith's self-mocking approach which allows her to
compare herself and her plight with past events of great
significance. This helps to create humour in the novel.

4 *Not drowning, but waving:* this refers to Stevie Smith's poem
'Not Waving but Drowning' in which the central figure
is thought to be fooling about when in fact he is crying
for help. The metaphor of the drowning represents his
inability to cope with life. The mistake is not realised until
it is too late. Edith is making the point here that with her
the opposite is true. While other people want to believe
her to be unable to cope, she is in fact perfectly all right.
tungsten: greyish-white metal used in lamp filaments.
nodded vestigially: gave the smallest sign of a nod.

5 *cypresses:* coniferous trees that have a very dark green
foliage, associated with graveyards.

6 *comme il faut:* the way it ought to be.

7 *guaranteed to provide a restorative sojourn:* it could be relied
upon to offer a resting place which would build up the
visitor's strength.
equable: even, unvarying.

8 *shelter without complicity:* he would accept them but he
disapproved, he would not be party to their wrongdoings.

10 *hiatus:* here this means a gap in time.

12 *someone of my benighted persuasion:* someone involved in dark-
ness. Edith is referring here to her writing of fiction. The
suggestion is that the writing of fiction distances her from
the real world.
an uncertain penumbra surrounding this odd pilgrimage: her
unexplained journey was surrounded by clouds of
uncertainty.

13 *Doomed for a certain time to walk the earth:* this refers to
Shakespeare's *Hamlet*. In most editions the line reads

149

'Doomed for a certain time to walk the night' and continues:

> And for the day confined to fast in fires
> Till the foul crimes done in my days of nature
> Are burnt and purged away.

(Act 4, scene 10)

Edith compares herself with the speaker, the ghost of Hamlet's father, who must continue to haunt and suffer until he has thus compensated for the crimes he committed whilst alive. This emphasises Edith's argument that her own behaviour has been considered a crime by her friends.

14 *Gotha:* the German equivalent of *Debrett* or Burke's *Peerage* – a list of the English nobility.

Chapter 2

15 *The Stone and the Star:* a reference to *Omar Khayyam* by Edward Fitzgerald.

> Awake! for Morning in the Bowl of Night
> Has flung the Stone that put the Stars to Flight:

Again, this adds to the sense of the romantic.

16 *Je vous en prie:* it's a pleasure.

Cosmopolitan: a magazine aimed at professional and semi-professional women in their late twenties and thirties.

17 *remarkably Bloomsburian:* like a member of the Bloomsbury group. This was a small, close group of intellectuals who lived in London in the early part of the twentieth century. Amongst them were Leonard Woolf and Virginia Woolf – a novelist with whom Edith Hope, to a certain extent, identifies.

the tortoise and the hare: this is one of Aesop's fables (see next note). In a race between them, the hare is so sure of his lead that he stops and sleeps. The tortoise keeps up an even pace and wins the race.

18 *Aesop:* a teller of animal fables who lived in the sixth century BC.

axiomatically: as a self-evident truth.

the tortoise lobby's propaganda: the group which tries to influence others through the way in which they put over information – in this case for the 'mouse-like unassuming girls'.

circumspect: watchful, careful.

The facts of life are too terrible to go into my kind of fiction: the truth about which women win the men, and how, is too difficult to face, and therefore out of place in the kind of romance written by Edith.

hucksters: people who sell their wares – a term of criticism. Edith suggests that certain people will make a profit out of anything, and she despises those who do it by writing for the 'hares'.

19 *Holland Park:* a wealthy area of west London.

20 *The Lady of Shalott:* a poem by Tennyson. The Lady is only allowed to look in her mirror and not at the outside world. When she does so, tempted by the sight of an attractive knight, she pays for the crime with her life. There is irony here in that Edith spends much of her time writing fiction, which is perhaps like looking in a mirror rather than at the real world.

crêpe de chine: a fine silk material which suggests expense.

21 *Frascati:* light Italian wine.

24 *Il fait froid?* is it cold?

Il a neigé cette nuit sur la montagne: last night snow fell on the mountain.

'Comment vous appelez-vous?': what is your name?

25 *Alain . . . Je m'appelle Alain:* Alain, my name is Alain.

the quotidian: the everyday.

26 *an embodiment of the kind of propaganda no contemporary woman could stoop to countenance:* Mrs Pusey represented

the kinds of ideals which present-day women utterly despise.

27 *a stolidity which verged on opulence:* a heaviness which was almost abundance – there was a lot of her.

28 *Haslemere:* a quiet country town on the border of Surrey and Sussex, well-known for its beautiful surroundings.
parquet floors: floors made out of pieces of wood arranged in a pattern.

29 *Cadenabbia:* a town on the edge of Lake Como, Italy.
Lucerne: Swiss resort.
Amalfi: Italian resort.
Deauville: resort in northern France.
Menton: resort in the South of France.
Bordighera: on the Italian riviera, just east of Menton.
Estoril: resort in Portugal.
Palma: resort in Majorca.

30 *Montreux:* Swiss resort on Lake Geneva.
Aladdin's cave: the reference to the old story suggests a mass of expensive possessions.

31 *to give herself a countenance:* to give herself moral support.
sybaritic: luxurious.

32 *duenna:* an older woman who acts as a chaperone.
the cut of Jennifer's jib: Jennifer's personal appearance.

33 *a solitary spree at the tables:* he went gambling on his own.
a closet member of the Marbella Club: he secretly visited the resort at Marbella, a place reserved for the rich and famous.

34 *Gustav Klimt:* an Austrian painter who lived from 1862 until 1918.
Schnitzler: an Austrian dramatist who wrote short plays which represented social problems.
Jugendstil: the German word for the art movement in the 1890s known as Art Nouveau (see note to page 55).
Schrecklich!: Terrible!
Ach du Schreck!: Oh, my God!
Kunsthistorisches Museum: Museum of Fine Art.

this is when character tells: this is the kind of situation which tests the moral qualities of people. Only the strong do well.

35 *fantasy and obfuscation:* fanciful invention and blocking out the real world – in other words, hiding its sadder side from herself and others.

Chapter 4

36 *Ouchy:* a place on the north side of Lake Geneva, east of Lausanne.

highly charged with vicarious emotion: tense and emotional as a result of experiencing feelings at second hand; that is, through writing about them.

38 *an effortless testimonial:* obvious proof of.

gamine: Jennifer dressed to give the image of a tomboy or impish child.

'They imposed their past ... homage': they forced you to become involved in both their past and their present, both of which you were expected to respect.

39 *requisitioned her:* pressed her into service.

uninflected: expressionless.

40 *the intrusion of a man into her consciousness, however parodic:* she was forced to be aware of a man, however poor an imitation he was of the one she wanted to be with.

Delacroix: French painter (1799–1863). Leader of a Romantic school of painting.

hammam: a Turkish bath.

41 *accomplished in venery:* well-practised in the art of hunting (men).

44 *gyneceum:* the women's apartment in a house.

45 *Virginia Woolf:* a writer from the Bloomsbury group, mentioned in note to page 17. As a novelist, she tried out a number of new techniques which are still used by writers today.

Chapter 5

47 *apostasy:* literally means abandonment of religion – here it means the casting aside of morally correct behaviour.

48 *febrile:* feverish.

'Embroiled in her fictional plot . . . exert no control: Edith was caught up in her own imaginary stories deliberately, so that she could escape the parts of reality that she could not change.

49 *Henry James:* American novelist (1843–1916) who settled in Europe from 1875. He wrote in a detailed and dense style which, in some novels, needs close and careful study in order to be understood and appreciated.

Ces Plaisirs, qu'on nomme, à la légère, physiques: 'The Pleasures which One Would Lightly Call Physical' (ironically referred to again on page 146), a volume of short stories written by the French novelist Colette (1873–1964). Her unusual ways of presenting relationships caused some scandal when her novels were first published.

50 *clothed in white samite, mystic, wonderful:* this is a quotation from Tennyson's *Idylls of the King, The Passing of Arthur.* The hand which takes back the sword Excalibur into the Lake is described by this line. Just as this hand returned the sword to its rightful place, so Edith imagines that Mrs Pusey can – by some spiritual power – dictate an order of events in her life.

52 *Eh bien, maman:* so, mother.

53 *croupier:* a person dealing and collecting cards for a gambling game.

oblique: devious.

54–5 *I'm a romantic . . . Love means marriage to me . . . Romance and courtship go together:* look back at your notes from While you are reading – Romance (page xxii). Decide which meaning best fits Mrs Pusey's words.

55 *Art Nouveau:* literally, in French, the new art. A style of art which was in vogue from about 1880 to 1910 and

which tended to use flowing curves and the kinds of shapes that are found in nature, for instance of plants and animals, as part of the design.

rebarbative: unattractive.

56 *lay figure:* not professional; Edith thinks of herself as a kind of extra who can be dispensed with on the arrival of someone more skilled.

57 *deconstruct the signifiers of your discourse:* literally, analyse the messages you are communicating. Philip Neville means that he could work out what Edith was thinking and feeling from looking at the expression on her face.

On s'en va?: shall we go?

J'arrive: I'm just coming.

58 *odalisque:* a woman from an Eastern harem.

Chapter 6

60 *I am subject to a certain amount of balkanisation:* the Balkan states (roughly the area now occupied by Bulgaria, Romania, Yugoslavia and Albania) were, until the First World War, subject to political alliances and takeovers by opposing powers, while struggling to gain their own independence. Whichever neighbouring country invaded the Balkan States proved its power by so doing. Mrs Pusey and Monica score points off each other by claiming Edith as their own particular companion or ally against the other.

60–1 *Her noble husband . . . arrangements:* if Monica cannot change the fact that she is unable to conceive a child, then her husband will get rid of her and find himself someone who can.

61 *prescient:* with foreknowledge, prophetic.

a remittance woman: someone to whom money is sent, on the understanding that she will not come home.

hieratic: priest-like.

that portrait of the Duke of Wellington: she is referring to a painting by Francisco del Goya in 1812. Set against a dark background and wearing a number of decorations, Wellington looks very sombre, rather proper – but slightly dazed.

62 *meek and complaisant:* submissive and polite.

foil: someone to set her off as a result of the comparison between them. Monica wishes to be in Edith's company, not because of Edith's personal qualities but for her role in showing off her own strengths.

narcissism: love of oneself.

63 *salacious:* lewd, thinking about sex.

déshabillés: nightgowns.

64 *Très portée sur la chose:* obsessed by it.

67 *Francesco Furini:* (1600–46), one of the most distinctive Florentine painters of the seventeenth century.

'I have taken the name of Virginia Woolf in vain': This is a reference to Virginia Woolf's thoughts at the end of her book about women and writing, *A Room of One's Own*. She had intended to conclude with 'something particularly disagreeable.' She changed her mind because, 'the truth is, I often like women'. Edith Hope, who identifies with Virginia Woolf (even her pen name is *V*anessa *W*ilde) feels guilty that she is not more tolerant of the women in the hotel. She imagines that Virginia Woolf might have been kinder in the same situation.

You have made a false equation: you have got it wrong.

Chapter 7

70 *sycophants:* flatters.

jongleurs: travelling minstrels.

subterranean: beneath the surface. Edith means that much of what happens to her is in her mind, or else secret.

72 *The wild boy of Aveyron:* In 1800, in Aveyron in central France, a boy of about twelve years old was discovered who had lived on his own in the woods and was completely unaware of the way in which people in society behaved. Edith compares herself to him to show her complete inability to know how to behave.

73 *You are a romantic:* see While you are reading – Romance (page xxi).

to assume your own centrality: to see yourself as being more important than anyone else, at the centre of everything.

74 *altruism:* selflessness.

75 *implode:* burst inwards.

76 *the world well lost for love:* Edith is referring to Dryden's play *All For Love* which is subtitled *The World Well Lost*. The story is similar to that of Shakespeare's *Antony and Cleopatra*. It tells about the relationship between Antony and Cleopatra. Antony lost his status as leader of the Roman world because he spent so much time with Cleopatra, with whom he was passionately in love (see note to page 3).

Nietzschean directness: Nietzsche was a German philosopher who believed that human beings could be made perfect through self-assertion. Edith here is hoping that she sounds very assertive indeed. The irony here is that it is over something as unimportant as a pot of coffee. She then changes her mind to tea, anyway.

77 *You write about love. And you will never write anything different, I suspect, until you begin to take a harder look at yourself:* Philip Neville is suggesting that Edith will never be able to write about anything (to his mind) more important, until she is more self critical and, as a result, changes her own lifestyle.

crepitate: literally, to make a crackling sound. Here, it means to tingle.

157

Chapter 8

80 *a veritable miasma:* the suggestion is that the scent pollutes the atmosphere.

cloud of unknowing: this is the title of a fourteenth-century document written by an anonymous English monk whose aim was to help individuals to live better lives and to know God better, as a result of their day-to-day experience. God can be found in the 'cloud of unknowing'. This is clearly an ironic reference as, for Edith and her mother, it means bewilderment about life.

81 *peignoir:* dressing gown.

lapis lazuli: bright blue semi-precious stone.

baroque: massive and complex. Baroque was a style of art used in early seventeenth-century Italy.

84 *homogeneous assembly:* a gathering of people all of whom are of the same type.

satirical intention: having the purpose or aim of ridiculing the Puseys.

85 *rite of passage:* ceremony or ritual which leads into a new stage in your life.

mutuality: intimacy.

86 *She knew from the outset . . . there may not be enough to go round:* this refers to one of the major themes of the novel; the difference between people like Edith and people like the Puseys who are more acquisitive, but perhaps happier.

87 *cornucopia:* overflowing store (literally, the horn of plenty).

a connoisseur of the fantastic, an intellectual voluptuary of the highest order: he knows a great deal about extraordinary matters, and takes an almost sensuous pleasure in the activities of the mind.

89 *Cranford:* a novel by Elizabeth Gaskell first published in 1853. It contains keen observations about village life, written in a gentle, witty style. The suggestion is that Edith talked to David about life in such a manner, rather than attempting to discuss her own feelings.

Chapter 9

93 *that illicit manufacture of a substance not needed for survival:*
Edith's job of writing is like a forbidden pleasure because
it is self indulgent and in no way practical.

96 *foundling:* infant deserted by its parents.

98 *Nesselrode pudding:* the original of this famous European
dessert was created by a court chamberlain in Belgium.
It is made from eggs, sugar, sherry and cream, with lady's
finger biscuits.

Chanel: famous dress designer.

99 *The Judgment of Paris:* this refers to a story from Greek
mythology. Paris, a Trojan youth, was asked to award the
Apple of Discord which was inscribed with the words 'To
the Fairest', to one of the three goddesses who had
claimed it – Hera, Aphrodite and Athene. He chose
Aphrodite who had bribed him with the offer of the
beautiful Greek, Helen, who was already married. The end
result was to create war between the Greeks and the
Trojans.

The suggestion is that Penelope, Edith and Mrs
Dempster each has a different style. Geoffrey would be too
well-mannered to choose between them, had he – like
Paris – been asked.

101 *the totality of his mouse-like seemliness:* an overall impression
of decency and dignity of a very timid, low-key kind.

102 *epic occurrence:* grand affair, full of heroic deeds.

Chapter 10

106 *prolonged reminiscence:* too lengthy a period of thinking
about the past.

108 *décolletage:* neckline.

109 *Imbécile!:* idiot.

Mais je n'ai rien fait: but I didn't do anything.

Madame . . . Dîtes leur. Je n'ai rien fait: Miss Hope. Tell them I didn't do anything.

111 *status quo:* the situation as it normally is.

112 *Edith felt eddies of disturbance . . . her more long lasting predicament:* the image is of a disturbance in a pool of water which spreads outwards. Edith felt upset by what had happened that morning. It seemed to have a bearing both on her existence in the Hotel du Lac and on more long-term problems.

mined (for hurt feelings): scrutinised.

113 *in that way the shadow of her mortality will be exorcised:* the knowledge that she is only human will have been cast out by the fact she has blamed other people.

brioche: a cake made with yeast.

115 *Honour is what David would call a busted flush:* A busted flush is an incomplete suit in a card game. This colloquial expression suggests that honour is a waste of time. Being honourable cannot achieve anything.

117 *the whole caboodle:* a colloquial expression meaning the works, the whole lot.

118 *only the possession of this day held worse at bay:* through making determined use of this day, they could keep their minds off the more difficult days in the future.

the seriousness of their respective predicaments . . . their own marginal existence: in the past, characters like Edith and Monica would have been objects of fun. However, now that they are beginning to take on even slightly more assertive roles, this makes it difficult for them to fit into society in the quiet way they always had.

sad precepts of a lost faith: rules for conduct which were no longer used because belief in them and their outcomes had been given up.

Le Soleil de Minuit: Edith's novel, *The Sun at Midnight* – translated into French (mentioned earlier).

119 *colloquies:* dialogues.

disaffection: estrangement.

120 *anachronistic:* literally means existing in the wrong historical period. The suggestion is that Edith and Monica are now definitely out of place at Haffeneggers. Their time for frequenting it is over.

their transitory nature, their fundamental unreality: their lack of permanence which made them cease to exist in the minds of the residents.

121 *refulgent:* radiant.

122 *réclame:* publicity, self-advertisement.

123 *Alors . . . Ça va mieux, la santé?:* 'So, you are recovered?'

Toujours pomponnée: always dressed up.

Chapter 11

124 *deerstalker hat:* cloth hat with peaks front and back, and ear flaps.

126 *persona:* assumed character.

their aimlessness raised to almost mythological status: their total lack of purpose seeming like a story or a parable.

127 *curiously mythological:* strangely unreal.

ingénue: innocent, an artless person.

129 *anodyne:* soothing.

Regency Gothic: a grand style of architecture used in the early nineteenth century.

famille rose dishes: antiques; the dishes are from Chinese ceramics produced around 1730 and coloured in pinks and brilliant reds.

130 *(you are never going to learn) the rules:* how to behave in order to get the best for yourself out of society and relationships.

Chapter 12

136 *the hair shirt of the penitent:* the coarse garment worn by people who had offended against the laws of the Church,

designed to cause discomfort and shame.

a valedictory hand: a wave of farewell.

137 *pension:* small hotel.

138 *totemic significance:* like an emblem.

140 *enigmatic:* puzzling, harbouring mystery.

reciprocity: mutual giving and receiving.

143 *fiasco:* total failure.

I am, as Swann said of Odette, not your type: this is a reference to *Remembrance of Things Past* by Marcel Proust. Odette is not Swann's type of woman, and their relationship damages his status in society. However, he is obsessed by her, she becomes his mistress and then, unlike David and Edith, he marries her. The reference to Proust is ironic. The relationship between Swann and Odette becomes official in marriage. The relationship between Edith and David never will.

Coursework assignments

There is a range of different types of work here. The first task is an oral one. Your teacher may feel it useful to assess this particular piece. Other assignments ask for written work, but it might help you to discuss a task before you begin writing.

As a general rule, the tasks marked 'Personal response' will be suitable for your English folder, and the ones marked 'Critical and Analytical' will be suitable for your English Literature folder. Some assignments may be acceptable in either folder. If you are in doubt, you should consult your teacher.

You do not need to complete every written assignment suggested here. You should select the activities which you will most enjoy. You need to include a variety of types of writing in your folders. If, therefore, you are short of a particular kind of writing, for example a playscript, or a piece of writing which uses information to express a point of view, then you should choose according to that need.

Personal response

Assignment 1: role play

Role play the conversation that took place between Penelope Milne and Mrs Dempster (a) on the day of the wedding, or (b) after Penelope had taken Edith to the airport.

Look back at pages 97, 99 and 103 in order to get some ideas.

Assignment 2: screen play

In a larger group, discuss the part of the novel which you would most like to present as a video.

163

You should choose a small section as there is a lot for you to do with it.

Write the screen play, bracketing the details of your characters' actions. Make sure these are clear and possible to do. For example:

EDITH [speaks in ringing tones] And what is the most potent myth of all?

Decide on the setting and write detailed notes about it. Write a list of any props that will be needed.

Draw out the storyboard (see below) and label the types of shot to be used.

Write notes for the actors and actresses about their tone, movement, manner, gestures and particular words and phrases to emphasise.

Write instructions for costume and make-up departments. If you have access to a video, you could tape this.

The series of small boxes drawn out for you opposite by the BBC School Broadcasting Council is an example of a storyboard. Each box is called a frame. The types of shot which you can use are also listed for you.

Assignment 3: radio play

If you prefer, you could write the same section of the novel for performance on radio.

Remember to think about sound effects. Remember to emphasise tone of voice in your instructions for actors and actresses. Tape it.

If others in the class are doing the same work, you could listen to another group's work. Comment on their choice of extract; comment on the changes which were made in order to ensure that the extract was suitable for performance on the radio.

Shot 1   *Shot 2*

Distance from subject

Shots are classified by the amount of a person taken in:

1 Extreme close-up (Detail shot) – isolated detail.

2 Very close-up (Face shot) – from mid-forehead to above chin.

3 Big close-up (tight CU, full head) – full head height nearly fills screen.

4 Close-up – just above head to upper chest (cut below necktie knot).

5 Medium close-up (bust shot, chest shot) – cuts body at lower chest (breast-pocket, armpit).

6 Medium shot (mid-shot, close medium shot, CMS, waist shot) – cuts body just below waist.

7 Knee shot, three-quarter length shot – cuts just below knees.

8 Medium long-shot (full length shot, FLS) – entire body plus short distance above/below.

9 Long shot – person occupies ¾ to ⅓ screen height.

10 Extra long shot (XLS), extreme LS.

Point of view shot

Usually two shots are used for this. Shot 1 shows a character looking away from the camera, out of shot. Shot 2 shows the object, person or scene which the viewer is supposed to imagine the character is looking at.

You can also do a point of view shot by making the camera appear to look through binoculars, a gunsight, a periscope etc.

Inside Television, BBC Enterprises, 1986

Assignment 4: *parents and children*

Edith says of her mother 'She had bequeathed to me her own cloud of unknowing' (page 80).

Her father's phrase, 'You have made a false equation, Edith,' is one that she remembers often (for example, page 67).

Write about the influences parents have on their children, showing how their habits and views affect their children's lives.

You may wish to write about yourself or someone you know, or you could choose to make up a character or characters.

Assignment 5: *that is how I tried to be*

'For that is how he saw me, she thought, and out of love for him that is how I tried to be' (page 89).

Edith tried to be the sort of person that David imagined her to be.

(a) Write a letter to Edith explaining why such behaviour is foolish and harmful to herself and her relationship;

or

(b) write your own story with this quotation as a title, showing what happens if you try to behave in the way you think someone wants you to.

Assignment 6: *newspaper article*

Imagine you have been asked by the local press to cover Edith's wedding to Geoffrey Long.

Write a short article for the front page of your paper, describing what happened.

or

You are Geoffrey Long. Write two poems:
  (a) on the night on which you gave Edith the ring
  (b) when she left for the Hotel du Lac.

Assignment 7: different views of a writer

Anita Brookner shows us a month in the life of one particular writer, and makes it clear what her personality is like. (You may like to look again at 'While you are reading: Edith Hope, note 2.) She wants us to change our stereotypical view of writers.

*Write a paragraph, giving a detailed caricature of a stereotypical writer. Then write a longer piece **either** describing someone you know who is a writer **or** describing in detail a writer who you have read about, seen on television, or heard about on the radio. Try to give a more balanced account of their appearance and personality.*

Assignment 8: invent a game

The purpose of the game is to show the successes and failures in Edith's life as we see it in the novel.

Your game could be like Snakes and Ladders. Instead of throwing a die, you could shuffle cards and select one. The cards might tell you what has happened to Edith and why that is a success or failure. (It might be a bit of both.) (See page 168.) You may use your own ideas about how to set this out.
  (i) Give your game a name;
 (ii) Draw out the board which should be used;
(iii) Write out the rules of the game;
(iv) Draw out the cards and any other items which will be of use in the game.

You ask Penelope to help you select the colour scheme for your bedroom.

GO DOWN 5

You do not feel comfortable with the colours.

The Puseys ask you to join them on your first evening at the Hotel du Lac.

GO UP 3

This is 'deliverance from the evening that lay ahead'.
But

GO DOWN 1

with them there is no 'reciprocity'.

Assignment 9: advice

A number of people in the novel give Edith advice.

Write a play script in which advice is given and expected to be found useful.

Demonstrate the outcome for the character(s) who are expected to make use of it. (The play script could be humorous or serious.)

Assignment 10: letters to Edith

Look very closely at the advice which Edith has received in her life from: her father; Harold Webb; Penelope; Mrs Pusey; Mr Neville.

Write Edith a letter in which you refer to the advice given by each of them.

Point out the usefulness and/or limitations of each piece you

Monica – pages 8–9, 20, 53
Iris Pusey – pages 9–10, 22, 26, 63
Jennifer – pages 38–9, 58.

Look carefully at some of these or others of your own choice. Decide what it is that makes them so successful and makes notes as you go along. You may like to make mention of the following:

– choice of situation in which we observe them;
– how the writer lets them behave with people and animals;
– what the writer lets them say;
– use of metaphor (a metaphor is a comparison which does not use the word 'like'; good metaphors help us to imagine or visualise what the writer wants us to see – for example, 'A tall woman . . . with the narrow nodding head of a grebe.');
– use of unusual words and phrases;
– originality;
– your own response to them and why they affect you in the way they do.

You may find useful the second part of the Introduction and the work from While you are reading on the Puseys and David.

(a) Using your notes, write an assignment called 'Character Creation in Hotel du Lac.'

or

(b) Write a series of descriptions of your own, imitating Anita Brookner's style. You can make up your own title.

Assignment 6: Parents and children in Hotel du Lac

Make a study of all the parent/child relationships mentioned in Hotel du Lac. *What, if anything, have you learned from these?*

mention, giving careful reasons for your opinions. Use quotations, but try to let them flow smoothly into your own sentences. For example:

Your publisher Harold has suggested to you that 'the romantic market is beginning to change'. You may not agree with him. . . .

Reread Chapter 9; remember Penelope's dominance. Then write the letter which Penelope might have sent to Edith soon after Edith had arrived at the Hotel du Lac. Write Edith's reply – on a postcard, if you like.

Critical and analytical

Assignment 1: marriage

'Marriage, they scorned, thinking of it as a shackle that kept women at home.' This is a quotation from Anita Brookner's novel *The Misalliance* (Jonathan Cape, 1986, page 28).

Do you consider that attitudes to marriage in the modern world have changed? Write an essay in which you investigate this.

You might like to look at:
– divorce statistics;
– the changing position of single and unmarried parents;
– whether men and women want the same thing from marriage;
– the concept of spinsterhood;
– views about open marriages;
– the mood of the times.

Assignment 2: Edith's suitors

Edith nearly married Geoffrey Long, and then, a few months later, Philip Neville.

(a) Describe these two men or draw them.

Give them clothes, expressions, gestures which you think are typical; label each of these details, giving short quotations or page references to the parts of the novel which give you this information.

(b) Write a short essay contrasting the two men and their behaviour, and commenting on their suitability as partners for Edith.

You may find this easier to do if you worked on 'Predicting the story', note 2 (page xxi).

Assignment 3: Edith

(a) Draw Edith's head and divide it into different areas. Write in the various aspects of Edith's personality in proportion to how they appear to you from reading the book.

Note an example or page reference alongside each reference. Your notes from While you are reading: The opening chapter, note 2b, and Edith Hope, notes 1a and 1b may help you.

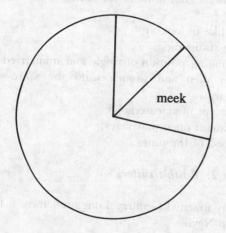

Anita Brookner uses a number of methods in order to sh
Edith's personality:
- the narrator's voice;
- presenting her reactions in a particular situation;
- writing as though she *is* Edith thinking;
- the letters to David;
- what she is allowed to say to others;
- the choice of vocabulary with which to describe her and her actions, e.g. 'her long narrow feet *tamed* into plain kid pumps';
- her clothes – small details like the cardigan that Mr Neville so objects to.

(b) Either using the entire book, or one particular chapter where a number of these devices can be seen, write an essay entitled 'Anita Brookner's Characterisation of Edith Hope'.

Assignment 4: Edith's stories

Of her stories, Edith tells David:
  'I believed every word I wrote. And I still do, even though I realise now that none of it can ever come true for me.' (page 144)

Describe the type of story Edith writes. Then say why the above statement is or is not true for her as we see her in the novel. Give reasons for your answer.

You may like to use your work from While you are reading: Edith Hope, note 3b.

Assignment 5: character creation in Hotel du Lac

Anita Brookner is particularly skilled at creating character. Here are some examples:

Assignment 7: creation of atmosphere

Through meticulous care over choice of words and phrases, Anita Brookner creates the moods of her characters and exactly the right atmosphere for the events which occur.

In a small group, or on your own, decide which of the following statements will be useful for you when writing an assignment about creation of atmosphere.

You should have in front of you a few of the following passages, some of which will be very short:
  - Edith's room at the Hotel du Lac (pages 2–3)
  - Edith and Philip Neville outside a small restaurant (page 69)
  - the morning of the wedding (pages 93, 97–8)
  - Edith's perception of her home area when she is on the way to the Registry Office (pages 100–1)
  - Monica and Edith at Haffenegger's (page 120).

Statements to help you

  - Long and complicated sentences help to emphasise wistfulness or confusion.
  - Use of short sentences gives an abrupt feeling to the passage and can suggest tension or misery.
  - Lists of several adjectives one after the other can help to build up a very clear impression of what is being described.
  - Certain words and phrases can suggest approval or disapproval in the person who is viewing the scene.
  - Repeated use of a particular colour as part of a description can suggest either a dullness or a completeness about the surroundings.
  - Choice of words or phrases which are not usually used to describe a particular object or place draw our attention to what is being described.

173

- Reference to particular types of weather help to create mood, for example a storm might emphasise the fact that the characters have strong feelings.
- Descriptions of sounds or lack of them create atmosphere.
- Descriptions of smells, pleasant or unpleasant, help to create atmosphere.
- use of similes (comparisons where 'like' or 'as' are used – for example, the clouds looked like candy floss) and use of metaphors.

Choose two or three passages and make detailed comments about them in response to the above title. You do not have to choose the ones suggested here unless you want to do so.

Assignment 8: 'unimportant novels'

Her novels are 'quite nice but unimportant'. This is what Anita Brookner told Simon Banner who was writing an article about her on the *Guardian* Women's Page, which is copied for you here.

Write a letter to the Guardian, *explaining what you agree with and what you disagree with in this statement.*

Amongst other things, you might like to talk about
- what *Hotel du Lac* shows about human nature;
- what it tell us about morality and scruples;
- what it has to say of importance about women.

Assignment 9: Hotel du Lac – *the film*

Christopher Hampton wrote the screen play for the BBC's adaptation of the novel for television. If you have been able to see this, then write a review for the Guardian, *showing how successfully you consider the film conveys the story and mood of the novel.*

174

'I DON'T know what people do when they do nothing; I'm not very good at leisure,' admits Anita Brookner. What she does when she might be doing nothing is to write novels – five, in fact, in the five years since she began writing. The fifth, Family and Friends (Cape, £8.95) is published tomorrow, and she is already working on the next.

That the publication of Family and Friends is one of the most keenly awaited events of the literary calendar cannot be in doubt. Nor the reason for all the attention. Anita Brookner won last year's Booker McConnell Prize with Hotel du Lac and overnight the modest, yet distinguished, art historian became a literary celebrity, while her novel climbed to the top of the best-seller lists on both sides of the Atlantic. 'They think I'm a nutter in America,' Dr Brooker says. But the book goes on selling.

Hotel du Lac is an aggressively uneventful novel: amid the soporific atmosphere of a Swiss hotel at the end of the season, a middle-aged romantic novelist reflects on her life back home in London. To say the least, not very much happens. Which made the novel something of an unlikely choice for the Booker prize: judging from previous winners the archetypal Booker novel would be an epic work offering liberal amounts of sex, violent incident, history, anguish, the odd intimation of apocalypse, and so forth. It was that sort of calculation which made J. G. Ballard's Empire of the Sun look like the winner last year. But Anita Brookner took the prize with hardly a hint of bad weather on the lake, let alone the apocalypse.

In that sense Family and Friends will come as no surprise. It offers more of those pleasures already familiar to admirers of her work: the self-conscious literariness of the writing; that eye and ear for the way language, dress and manners betray character and class; the sharpness of the wit; the amusing but dreadful inexorability of personal fate. The sort of critic who judged Hotel du Lac to be 'a classic, a book which will be read with pleasure a hundred years from now,' will not be disappointed with Family and Friends.

Those who see Anita Brookner as 'one of the great writers of contemporary fiction' will have their opinion confirmed.

Dr Brookner herself better remembers those hostile to her winning the Booker Prize. 'The press here is quite brutal,' she says. Malcolm Bradbury complained that Hotel du Lac was 'parochial,' not at all the sort of book which should have won Britain's most prestigious literary award. The New Statesman rubbished the book and the author along with it, as 'pretentious,' recalling, however, that it wasn't her 'fault that she won the prize.'

Quite. In the row that blew up last autumn, Anita Brookner admits that she 'wanted to go round saying: look, I didn't award this to myself!' She thinks it would have been better for everyone concerned if J. G. Ballard's Empire of the Sun had won. 'People would have been pacified in some way.' Like her own famous heroine, Edith Hope, she makes no claims 'for my particular sort of writing.' Her novels, she thinks, are 'quite nice, but unimportant.'

The Guardian, 4 September 1985

Assignment 10: biased?

Some women writers have been accused of giving a biased view of men in their novels. In *Hotel du Lac* we meet

Harold Webb
Geoffrey Long
Philip Neville
David Simmonds
Alain
Monsieur Huber

Reference is also made to the behaviour and opinions of Mr Pusey, Monica's husband and Mme de Bonneuil's son.

Write an essay explaining how far you consider the accusation of bias to be true of Hotel du Lac.

First jot down notes of anything the men have in common, their strengths and weaknesses. Then you need to decide whether or not this group show us what men are really like.

Comment also on the types of women presented here in the novel. This will help you to ask if Anita Brookner is or is not more sympathetic towards women than men.

Assignment 11: how should people treat one another?

Read these statements on the various characters in the novel.

Mrs Pusey:

'She knew from the outset what some unfortunates never learn. She knew that the best is to be taken, although there may not be enough to go round.' (page 86)

Edith:

'It is I who am at fault, she thought. It is because I am so meek that people fail to notice my demands. Or it is even more simple than that. I fail to make them.' (page 115)

Mr Neville:

'I am not in the business of losing *my* centrality'. (page 134)

What message does the novel offer us about how people should treat one another?

Remember to look carefully at the views which each one of the characters has, and the consequences of their behaviour for themselves.

or

Edith's mind works on 'the question of what behaviour most becomes a woman'. The novelist shows us several women who behave in very different ways.

Make a careful study of the women and their behaviour, and then explain clearly what kind of behaviour you think Anita Brookner most approves of and say why you think this.

Assignment 13: humour

Despite its seriousness, and the predicament of its heroine, *Hotel du Lac* is a very humorous book, poking fun at the society which it chooses to describe.

(a) Choose a number of passages and read them aloud. Explain to a small group how the humour works in each case.

This could count as one of your oral assessments.

(b) Write an essay called 'Humour in Hotel du Lac'.

The following words and examples might be of use to you.
  - satire: holding up for ridicule particular human qualities (e.g.: the Puseys' greed).
  - irony: writing in which the meaning is often the opposite

of the feelings expressed (e.g. page 93 – 'She was lucky. I am lucky, she reminded herself.').

– juxtaposition: the placing of one phrase alongside another ensures a humorous result (e.g. page 27 – '. . . everything that Mrs Pusey had said so far was of the utmost triviality. Clearly there were depths here that deserved her prolonged attention.').

Find your own examples of these:

repetition

exaggeration/caricature

situation comedy

unexpected behaviour from a character you thought you knew.

Remember to show your responses to such humour.

Assignment 14: romantic? (see While you are reading – 'Romance', page xxi)

In a small group, discuss the following statements:

Hotel du Lac is a romantic novel;

The novel *Hotel du Lac* is anti-romantic.

You may like to write this up for an assignment. You might find it useful to focus on some of these issues:

– the definition of 'romantic';

– the meanings which various characters give to this word;

– the setting of the novel. How far is it meant to be 'romantic'?

– Edith's novels. In what way are they 'romantic'?

– Edith's relationships with Geoffrey Long and Philip Neville;

– Edith's relationship with David. In what sense could it be called a 'romantic' relationship? Is it a realistic relationship?

– Jennifer's encounters with men. Would you describe these as 'romantic'?

- the different marriages we hear about in the book. What can be learnt from these about Anita Brookner's attitude towards marriage?
- Mr Neville's attitude to marriage;
- Anita Brookner's opinion. Does she think most like Edith, or is her opinion more similar to Mr Neville's?

Wider reading

If you have enjoyed reading *Hotel du Lac*, you may like to try some of the six other novels that Anita Brookner has written. These are:

A Start in Life
Providence
Look at Me
Family and Friends
The Misalliance
A Friend from England

Here are some other books that you might enjoy:

Lady Oracle by Margaret Atwood
Pride and Prejudice and *Northanger Abbey* by Jane Austen
My Brilliant Career by Miles Franklin
The Albatross and other stories by Susan Hill
Heat and Dust by Ruth Prawer Jhabvala
(The last three books are in the Modern Women Writers series.)

The exercises which follow are intended for use in the Wider Reading, Independent Reading or the Project section of your syllabus. I have suggested novels and a short story which cover similar themes or issues, so that you can look at the different ways in which writers present these. You are not expected to attempt all of these. You might choose one

to work on, and then read the other novels mentioned for
pleasure.

Assignments

1 What similarities do you find between the main characters
in *Providence* and *Hotel du Lac* and their fates? What do you
think is Anita Brookner's attitude towards her heroines?

2 Make a study of the statement 'the good live unhappily ever
after' (*Family and Friends*, Triad Panther, 1986, page 183) in
relation to two or three of *Hotel du Lac, Family and Friends,
Providence* and *The Misalliance*.

3 Compare the ways in which the heroines of *Providence* and
A Start in Life handle or mishandle relationships and find
reasons from your reading of the novels for why this might
be so.

4 Look carefully at the reasons why Edith Hope in *Hotel du
Lac* and Sybilla in *My Brilliant Career* turn away offers of
marriage (more than one in each case), and consider the
consequences of these decisions.

5 Show how two or three of the following texts present people
who feel they are missing out on some of what life has to
offer, and their attempts to seek for more: *Hotel du Lac*, 'Cockles
and Mussels' (from *The Albatross and other stories*) and
Providence.

6 Write an appreciation of how the setting and the way it is
described add to our enjoyment of the story in two of the
following: *Hotel du Lac, My Brilliant Career* and *Heat and
Dust*.

7 'I won't write any more Costume Gothics, though; I think
they were bad for me.' *Lady Oracle*, Seal Books, McClelland
and Stewart Bantam Limited, 1979 (page 345). Consider

the effects of the writing of romantic fiction on the lives of Edith Hope in *Hotel du Lac* and Joan Foster in *Lady Oracle*.

8 What attitudes to marriage do you find in *Pride and Prejudice* by Jane Austen and in *Hotel du Lac* by Anita Brookner?

Longman Study Texts **General editor: Richard Adams**

Titles in the series:

Plays

Novels and stories

Jane Austen
  Emma
  Pride and Prejudice
Charlotte Brontë
  Jane Eyre
Emily Brontë
  Wuthering Heights
Charles Dickens
  Great Expectations
  Oliver Twist
George Eliot
  Silas Marner
  The Mill on the Floss
Nadine Gordimer
  July's People
Thomas Hardy
  Far from the Madding Crowd
  The Mayor of Casterbridge
  Tess of the d'Urbervilles
Aldous Huxley
  Brave New World
Robin Jenkins
  The Cone-Gatherers
D H Lawrence
  Sons and Lovers
Somerset Maugham
  Short Stories
George Orwell
  Animal Farm
  Nineteen Eighty-Four
Alan Paton
  Cry, The Beloved Country
Paul Scott
  Staying On
Mark Twain
  The Adventures of Huckleberry Finn
H G Wells
  The History of Mr Polly
Virginia Woolf
  To the Lighthouse

Oliver Goldsmith
  She Stoops to Conquer
Ben Jonson
  Volpone
Christopher Marlowe
  Doctor Faustus
J B Priestley
  An Inspector Calls
Terence Rattigan
  The Winslow Boy
Willy Russell
  Educating Rita
Peter Shaffer
  Amadeus
  Equus
  The Royal Hunt of the Sun
William Shakespeare
  Macbeth
  The Merchant of Venice
  Romeo and Juliet
Bernard Shaw
  Androcles and the Lion
  Arms and the Man
  Caesar and Cleopatra
  The Devil's Disciple
  Major Barbara
  Pygmalion
  Saint Joan
Richard Brinsley Sheridan
  The Rivals
  The School for Scandal
John Webster
  The White Devil
  The Duchess of Malfi
Oscar Wilde
  The Importance of Being Earnest

Editor: George MacBeth
  Poetry for Today
Editor: Michael Marland
  Short Stories for Today